MOLLY

THE PALMER SISTERS BOOK 7

KAYT MILLER

CONTENTS

 Created with Vellum

Hopeful Romantic (Link coming soon.)

Thanks to Margie Dill (Link coming soon.)

To all of those who serve or have served in the armed forces, and their families, thank you.

CHAPTER ONE

Molly

"HAPPY BIRTHDAY, dear Madalyn, happy birthday to you."

I'm singing along, but my mind is on other things. *Like the fact our little girl is three. And that you're not here, Adam.*

She's so much like him.

She looks like me, sure, but everything that makes her a special little person is all you, Adam. God, I wish you were here.

I do my best to shake off my thoughts. As soon as the song ends, we all clap. I take the opportunity to look around the extra-large table we've got set up at Gustafson Custom Motorcycles, more specifically in Keeton's showroom—or brag room, as my little brother Eric calls it. It fits. Ordinarily, the room is filled with my big brother's awards, framed magazine covers in which he's featured, and one or two custom motorcycles.

But not today. No, today almost everything has been cleared out to make room for my baby girl's third birthday party. We needed space since our family, which started off as just my two brothers and me, has expanded to include the Palmer clan, the entire Gustafson Custom Motorcycle family, and numerous friends of all of us. It's blown up in the last couple of years to ten times the size we were when my Maddy was born.

I see my brother Eric first. He's holding his son, Oliver, who is just six months old. His wife, Violet—the sweetest person on earth—is cooing at her baby next to him. I smile because I'm happy for them. My brother is a great guy and an even better father. I'm so proud of him I could burst.

I search the crowd for Keeton, the oldest in our family. When I spot him, he's on the floor in the play area he and Lainie set up when their little girl, Rachel, was old enough to come to the shop now and then. Now she's two and a handful. Not only that, she's got her daddy wrapped around her pretty little finger. Case in point: Keeton, my big, bad biker brother, is wearing dark jeans, a black T-shirt with a skull on the front, leather biker boots, and a tiara. No joke. A tiara. That's what he does for his girl. Or I guess I should say girls because his wife is Lainie belongs on the list. She's wonderful and sweet and amazing and Violet's older sister. It doesn't seem possible that one family could produce two such genuinely kind people, but it turns out it produced five. Well, correction. Keely is an acquired taste, but she's still funny as hell and cool. I like her spunkiness.

I blink when I realize I've been staring at my brother playing with Rachel. I watch as Lainie moves closer with her palm on her stomach. She's pregnant again, due sometime in the spring. My brother has it all. He really does. And he doesn't take it for granted. Neither of my brothers do. They know how fragile and unpredictable life can be. One minute you're happily married awaiting the arrival of your child, and, BAM, the next thing you know your husband is dead a week before her birth.

No. I can't start that kind of thinking. Not today of all days.

Adam died three years ago in Afghanistan. He died doing what he loved—serving his country. Granted, he was getting out so he could be here with me and Maddy, but he loved his job.

Shit. My eyes burn a little bit, but, goddammit, I'm not going to get all maudlin on Maddy's big day. We've been planning this party for weeks. Her theme is based on her favorite Disney character. No, it's not a princess. It's a horse. Maximus from the movie *Tangled*. She loves that horse, and I don't blame her. He was hilarious. So, yeah, Sadie, the middle Palmer sister and owner of Sadie Cakes Bakery, made her an amazing cake shaped like a horse, the walls are decorated in *Tangled* gear we bought at a party store, and she's never been happier. It could also be because she's surrounded by cousins, friends, aunts, and uncles. She's a social butterfly, so the attention she's getting today, along with too many presents and way too much sugar, is making her vibrate with giddiness.

"Hey, Molls."

I look over at another one of the Palmer sisters, Agatha. "Hey." I peek down at the little one on her hip. "Hey there, Lily," I say in my higher-than-normal mom voice. "You're getting so big."

"And stinky." Agatha pinches her nose with her free hand. "Mind if I use your office to change her?"

"Actually," I say as Lily holds on to my finger, "we've set up Lainie's office as a makeshift changing area. It's even stocked up with diapers, wipes, and a rocker."

"Oh my gosh. You're amazing," Agatha says with a huge smile. "Thanks."

"No problem." And it's not. It was actually Keeton's idea. Not only do we have the babies I've already mentioned, but we've also got Sadie and Charlie's little guy, Finn. He's nearly two as well. He and Rachel were born only a couple months apart. In addition to that, Polly and Cortland Ashbury have a newborn baby, Laura, named after his feisty grandmother. And even Keely is pregnant, due in July. There's one other person with similar news, but I promised to keep that a secret until she's further along.

"Mama," says my girl from her booster seat. She's completely covered in cake. Head-to-toe in cake.

"Yes, birthday girl?" I reach out and swipe some frosting from her cheek and put it in my mouth. "Mm, yummy."

"Mama," she giggles. "Don't eat my face."

I will never tire of hearing that giggle. Is there anything better than a child's laugh? Nope. I laugh as I reach for another taste. "But you're so delicious."

"Mommy. No!" she says in her demanding voice. The one I remember hearing a lot from her father. My Adam was bossy as all get-out, but he was the love of my life and I was his. He did everything he could to make me happy.

Everything but live, I guess.

"Okay, birthday girl. I won't eat your face. Are you ready to open presents?"

"Yeah!" she shouts at the top of her little lungs.

"Let's go get cleaned up." I brought a second outfit for her to wear for precisely this reason. Cake is her kryptonite.

"Okay." She hops down from her chair, places her gooey, cake-covered hand in mine, and off we go to the makeshift baby room.

CHAPTER TWO

Sig

IF YOU'D TOLD me ten years ago that I'd be standing around at a kiddy party talking with a local cop and a retired FBI agent, I'd have punched you in the throat for being a fucking idiot. Cops and I have never seen eye to eye on shit. Hell, the reason I joined the army was because I had to make a choice. As a juvenile delinquent and a repeat offender, the cops, along with my dad, strongly suggested I try the military. It was either that or end up in jail someday. I jumped at the army option even though I knew the army would be the hardest thing I'd ever do. And I'm not just talking physically.

So, yeah, here I am at a kiddy party, standing around with guys I'd easily call my friends. If my father could see this shit, he'd probably roll over in his grave. Not only do the pack of us do stuff like this together, but we fish, play poker, and hang out to watch a game now and then. So, yeah, they're my friends, and they have been for the past couple of years, ever since I moved to this sleepy little town.

And I've needed them.

When I left the service, I felt sort of empty inside, like part of me was gone. Hell, the minute I changed out of my army fatigues for the last time, I felt like I'd lost a limb. That is, until I came here. I walked into Gustafson Custom Motorcycles and met Keeton, a man I'd heard a great deal about, shook his hand, and suddenly felt better. Home.

Hell, I'm not going to get into all that bullshit now. I'll save that for another day. No, today is about Princess Maddy. I don't say that all bitchy either. She *is* a princess. She's, hands down, the prettiest little girl I've ever seen. And sweet? Damn, she's a sweetheart. And funny. The little girl cracks me up daily with all her silly questions and completely uninhibited observations. For instance, Maddy has informed me multiple times that I'm too tall, too hairy, and I need to smile more. Yeah, she's highly critical of me. She takes after her mama in that regard, that's for sure.

Speaking of her mama, I scan the room in search of her. I don't have to look far; she's talking to her daughter. I watch as she swipes frosting from her kid's cheek and places it in her mouth. Maddy laughs, which makes Molly smile. Not something that happens all that often.

"So, what'd you get my niece?" asks Eric Gustafson as he slaps me on my back.

"Drum set."

"Damn, what're they going to do with two of those?" snickers Eric.

"One at your place?" I smirk.

"Or at yours. You live right next door to her, and she hangs at your place more than she does mine; it makes more sense to put it there."

He's right. Maddy hangs out at my place every now and then so Molly can do girl shit. I'm not her regular babysitter by any means, but I'm there if she needs me.

"Well," I chuckle, "lucky for you, I wasn't an asshole. You'll have to wait and see what I got her."

I actually made her something. A wooden doll bed for her favorite toy. It rocks like a cradle. I carved the doll's name, Dolly, in the headboard and had a local seamstress make the bedding for it. I hope she likes it.

Eric turns just as his wife, Violet, steps up holding their baby boy. "Time to open gifts, guys. Can you all come over to the table?"

"Sure thing, honey," Eric says softly, reaching his arms out toward his baby. "Let me have my boy."

Violet raises him gently and places him in Eric's arms. They both stare at their kid, and I can't help but feel a pang of jealousy. I want that. I want *all* that.

CHAPTER THREE

Molly

"MADDY, honey, no. You can't take Dolly's bed to the store with you."

"Why not, Mommy?"

"For one, it's sort of heavy and two..." It's annoying. She loves that thing. It's by far her favorite birthday gift.

Of course it is.

"Unkee Thig made it. I want to bwing it."

"Maddy, I've told you. He's not your uncle."

I watch as her little chin starts to quiver. I do everything I can to contain the eye roll that's dying to come out. My little girl is a master manipulator. I swear she can make that chin quiver on command.

"Nope." I shake my head. "Not this time, Maddy. The bed stays home."

"But, Dolly ith thleepy."

"Then maybe Dolly should stay home too."

Oh, shit. That was the wrong thing to say. I watch, like it's in slow motion, as her face changes from pale pink to red. Big, wet tears begin to flow out of her eyes, and her chin is going nuts.

"Maybe Sig can babysit Dolly *and* the bed while we're gone."

Yep. That did it. Everything stops: the tears, the redness of her pretty face, and the quiver.

"Okay," she says, like nothing just happened.

"Fine," I huff. Picking up the bed, I take the two steps down off our porch and wait for her to follow me with Dolly. Marching across the two driveways, ours and his, I take two identical steps up to his front door. I wait for Maddy to ring the bell. She likes to do it, and I don't give a shit.

I watch as his door opens. His eyes go directly to Maddy. "What's up, Mad Max?"

He calls her Mad Max. I'm not sure why.

"Unkee Thig," she says with a cute little lisp. "Can you babythit Dolly?"

For the first time since he opened the door, Sig looks at me. His brow arches. I think he's waiting for an explanation, but I don't really have one. Wait, oh yeah, my kid is spoiled. But I'm unapologetic about that. People can go fuck themselves if they don't like it. She's been dealt a shitty hand. So, yeah, she's spoiled. Get over it.

I sigh. "Dolly's tired. We can't take the bed with us." I glare at him. I don't know why. It's just something I do a lot. At Sig. I glare, I smirk, I snarl, and I roll my eyes. I'm sure there's more, but we need to get on the road, so the rest will have to come later.

"Sure thing, Maddy." He opens his screen door. Reaching out, he takes the bed from my hands and holds the door open for Maddy. "Where do you think she should go?"

Maddy points to his large reclaimed wood coffee table.

While they arrange her bed, I take the opportunity to look around his place. It's the mirror image of my layout, but where I've got a wall between my living room and kitchen, his is open. I remember this house before he moved in, and there used to be a wall. *I wonder how hard that would be to do at my place?*

I feel little fingers slide into my palm. I look down at my smiling girl as she gives my hand a tug. "Leth go, Mama."

PULLING INTO MY DRIVEWAY, I glance back and see my baby girl sound asleep in her car seat. Shopping sure tuckers her out. Turning back toward my little 1930s Craftsman bungalow, something up on the roof catches my eye.

I feel my body tense instantaneously.

What is he doing now?

This guy drives me up the damn wall. He's always up my ass doing shit like this—one day I came home from a hair appointment and he was installing outdoor motion sensor lights on the side of my house. Another time, he decided all my windows needed caulking. And I don't know how many times I've caught him doing my yard work even though I've asked, no, I've *told* him multiple times to stop.

Closing my car door quietly, I stomp up to the side of my house, craning my neck so I can yell at Sig without waking Maddy up. "What the fuck are you doing on my roof?"

I suck in a deep breath. *Patience, Molly.* I stand with my hands on my hips and my right foot tapping on the ground, waiting impatiently for a response. When he doesn't answer me, I take a step back until I see him. All of him.

Shit, this pisses me off. Because I know for sure there's nothing wrong with my goddamn roof.

Looking back at my car, I can see Maddy's still sound

asleep. I left the car on for the air conditioning, so she'll be fine for a couple of minutes.

"Sig!" I snap. This guy drives me batshit crazy. Since he seems to be ignoring me, I repeat, louder this time, "What the fuck are you doing on my roof!?" I'm standing beneath the eaves on my house, close enough for him to hear me. "Sig!?" I snap again.

"What, babe? I'm kinda busy."

Kinda busy? WTF?

Why does he sound put out? Like *I'm* the one bothering *him*. "Get off my goddamn house!" I shout and stomp my foot so hard I accidentally kick the stone edging Sig installed one Saturday when I was in Flagstaff with the Palmer girls.

"Fuck," I mutter as I hop on one foot.

"You okay?" he asks, leaning over the side of the roof.

He's so far over, I'm positive his massive body weight will pull him down. "Jesus, be careful!" If he falls, he could sue me. He'd win even though I never gave him permission to get on my roof. "Sig. What are you doing?" My tone is not quite as snippy now. It's more of a whimpery whine, because my damn foot hurts now.

"Loose shingle. I noticed it last week. Finally had the time to fix it."

"Loose shingle? I never noticed a loose shingle."

Sig leans over the roof and chuckles in a deep, rumbling way he does. "Course not, babe."

"What's that supposed to mean?" I stomp again, this time careful not to jam my toe on the edging. "I take care of things."

"Jesus," he mutters. Then I hear him sigh from ten or twelve feet above me.

What's that? He's getting annoyed with *me*? "Join the club, asshole."

"Huh?" Sig says right next to my ear. I scream in surprise.

"How did you get down so fast?"

"Jumped."

"You jumped off my roof? That's so dangerous."

He gives me that look. You know the one, ladies. The one that makes it seem like you're an idiot and he can't figure out how to break it to you? Yeah, one of his red, bushy eyebrows is arched way up, and his mouth is slightly agape. "Babe."

"Stop calling me that." God, how many times have I asked him not to call me that? A million times. I don't want to hear it. Not from him. *Adam called me baby.* That endearment belongs to him.

"Sig," I say with the calmest voice I can manage. "Next time, if you see something that needs fixing, tell me. I'll take care of it."

"Why?"

"Why, what?"

"Why do I need to tell you when I'm perfectly capable of doing it?"

"Sig." My voice is now less calm. "This is my house." I point my thumb at my chest. "You have your own house." I point to the house directly west of mine. "Take care of yours and leave mine alone."

"Molly," he says softly. "What kind of man would I be if I didn't help my neighbor out now and then?"

I call bullshit. "Do you help old Mr. Talco?" I point to the house to his west. "He's way more helpless than I am." Wait, I'm not helpless. "I mean—"

"No. He's got children and grandchildren to help him out."

"I've got two brothers who..." are too busy to help me. "Well, they'd help if I asked."

"Sure, sure." He nods. "But I'm right here." This time he uses his thumb to point to his 1930s Craftsman bungalow. "Besides, my house is all done. Yours still needs a little TLC."

I gasp. Why does that offend me? It does need TLC. Maybe it's because Adam and I bought this house together. It was such a huge accomplishment. We were so proud of ourselves—being homeowners. We had plans to fix the place up. He'd send me ideas and sketches for our house in his letters from overseas.

His letters.

I haven't read his letters for so long. After he died, I read them constantly. I put them in chronological order so I could remember everything in the right sequence. Sure, we Skyped and emailed, but Adam felt like letters were much more personal and romantic. Emails get deleted. Letters are forever. *It's too bad he and I weren't forever.*

I'm shaken from my depressing thoughts by movement. Sig has started moving toward my car.

"She asleep?" he asks, loud enough for me to hear him as he moves.

"Yes." At least she was.

By the time he opens the door, I hear crying. "Oh, shit." I jog to the car and attempt to pass the big oaf.

"It's okay, Mad Max. We're here."

We're here?

"Dolly's been missing you."

"Dolly?" she asks through sleepy sniffles.

"She's been on the porch waitin' for ya."

I turn slowly and scan my front porch. Sure enough, he's got Dolly's bed on one of the wicker chairs. I smile. I can't help it, because the guy has a towel lying over the bed to protect Dolly from the elements.

I let Sig carry her up to the house so I can shut off my car. Popping the trunk latch, I move to the back of my car and start to pull out our shopping bags.

"Whoa, you really went all out. You havin' a party or something?"

"No. We were just out of everything." We went to a nearby Super Target—the one-stop shop for us. Maddy likes it there, mostly because there's a nice toy section. I admit that I bribe my baby girl—if she's good, she gets to pick out a small toy. I know. Spoiled.

"Looks like it." Sig reaches around me and picks up over half the bags with one go. Not surprising, the guy is all muscles and bulk. He's bigger than Adam was. Not by much, but he's definitely one or two inches taller and he has to outweigh him by twenty pounds.

"Go on, babe. Get Maddy. I'll bring these in and get out of your hair."

That'd be nice.

I guess.

CHAPTER FOUR

Sig

SITTING ALONE in my silent living room, I look around my place, wondering what to do. It's almost supper time; I could cook. Better yet, I could get something delivered. I sigh. I'm sick of takeout. Don't get me wrong—I'm a decent cook, but it sucks to cook just for myself. If the guys were coming over to watch a game or to play some poker, I'd have an excuse to make something.

I wonder what the girls are havin' for supper.

I sigh again. I can't help it. I want... I want... *them.* I've been patient—almost three fucking years patient. The time has never been right, though. I've always sensed her sadness—her mourning for her man. I get it. I do. But, enough is enough.

Running my hands through my unruly hair, I sigh for a third time. It's no good. She's not ready.

～

WHEN I HEAR light taps on my front door, I stand quickly. I recognize the knock. Looking around my place, I check to make sure everything is neat. I hate clutter. When I'm sure it looks good, I step to the door and open it quickly.

"Hey," I say as nonchalantly as possible.

"Hey," Molly says hesitantly.

"Hi, Thig," chirps Maddy.

"What's up?" I lean against the doorjamb, attempting to be cool.

"We got you dezthert," says Maddy, holding up a plastic container. "Fank you for babythitting Dolly."

"And dinner," Molly says, holding out a plate covered in plastic wrap.

Ah, I see. It's not for working on her roof. "Well, thank you," I say with way too much enthusiasm. I can't help it. I mean it. Pushing open the screen door, I motion for my two favorite girls to enter.

"We can't stay." Molly nods toward her daughter. "Bedtime," she adds, looking down at her little troublemaker.

"Sure." I take the container from Maddy and the plate from Molly. Lifting them slightly, I say, "I'll get these back to you."

"No hurry." Molly sounds tentative.

I'm not sure what to say, and apparently neither is Molly, because we just stand in silence. Thankfully, the little beauty breaks up the awkward. Jumping on my couch, she makes herself right at home, saying, "Wanna watch *Tangled*, Thig?"

Molly rolls her eyes, then turns to her look-alike. "No, Maddy. It's bedtime."

"No." Maddy crosses her little arms in front of her defiantly. "*Tangled.*"

"No." Molly mimics her daughter. "Bedtime." Before Maddy can rebut, she says, "We'll watch it tomorrow."

Maddy throws herself onto her back on my sofa. "Fine," she huffs.

Chuckling, I set the plate and dessert on my counter. "Come on, Mad Max. I'll carry you home."

"Piggyback?" she says, happy again.

"Sure." I turn so my back is in front of her, kneeling down. She jumps on me and wraps her little arms around my neck. "Hang on tight."

"Okay," she says with a giggle. "Gitty up, Maxthismus."

I guess I'm a horse now. No worries. I'll be anything for my girls.

CHAPTER FIVE

Molly

"JESUS. Why can't these guys write legibly?" I don't even have to ask which one of the guys wrote up this order. I've been office manager for my brother's bike shop for over five years now. I know everyone's handwriting, since I'm in charge of ordering equipment, supplies, and parts, doing payroll for a growing staff, plus I'm a therapist and a nurse to most of these guys. Whenever they've got an issue, they run into my office, and I do what I can to help them. Whether they're upset about a girl or they cut themselves pulling out a carburetor, I'm like their makeshift mom her at GCM. I don't mind. I kind of like it, to be honest. I like to feel needed. Sure, Maddy needs me; I'm her mom. But I like being needed by the people here. They're my family, and I'm theirs.

Standing up from my desk, I raise my arms above my head to get a good stretch in. I get tired of sitting on my ass all day long. I need to move now and then. Lord knows a little exercise would do me some good. My ass is spreading wider and wider every year, and it wasn't small to begin with. No matter. Who cares? No one is interested in this behind or anything else surrounding it. Who the hell wants a widow? Especially one who can't seem to get happy.

Grabbing the order form, I step out of my office. The first person I see is my sister-in-law Lainie. She's working in her small office across the hall. We all call it her writing room, since that's what she does in there. She writes romances. Good ones. Steamy ones. The only bad part is, I'm 99 percent sure she uses my brother as inspiration for the sexy stuff, and whenever one of those scenes start in the book, I have to skip it. Either that, or I have to throw up in my mouth a little bit.

"Hey, Lain. How's the new book coming along?"

Her head jerks up like she didn't know I was there. Her cheeks are sort of flushed red. I start to laugh, because I know what she was doing. "Writing something dirty, huh?"

"Uh, um, well..." Lainie giggles. "Yeah."

"It must be good. You're all flustered."

She shrugs and smiles. "Yeah. It's a hot one."

I'd love to tell her I can't wait to read it, but I don't want to know anything about my brother's appendage, if you know what I mean. A shiver runs through me as I wave to Lainie. "Off to find out what the hell this invoice says."

"Okay," she says, but she sounds lost in thought. Or lost in lust is more like it.

I chuckle to myself as I walk through Keeton's brag room and out the door to the shop. I scan the room in search of my neighbor. When I don't spot him, I yell at Eric, "Where's Sig?"

He looks up from working on a bunch of bike parts that are laid out on a long table. He's putting something back together—like a puzzle. "Sick." He shrugs. "Called in this morning."

Sick? I saw him a few days ago....

I roll my eyes. A person can get sick in less than a few days. "Okay."

I've turned to leave when Eric adds, "You should check on him."

I roll my eyes again, but my back is to him so he can't see. "Sure." I pause. "Maybe." I raise my hand and give my little brother a small wave. Time to get back to work.

TWO DAYS PASS, and Sig is still a no-show at work. Since everyone at work is worried about him, I decide to do my neighborly duty and check on the man. He does do a lot for us; it's the least I can do. Holding a container of chicken noodle soup, I tap on his front door. When no one answers, I tap again. Still no answer.

Pulling open his screen door, I reach for the doorknob, but his door pushes open. It wasn't latched or locked. Now I'm worried. Stepping through his open door, I scan the living room. He's not in this room. *Shit*. What if someone broke into his place? What if he's hurt? Or worse, d-e-a-d.

I gasp at the thought. My heart hurts just thinking about it. I can't figure out why, though. There's nothing between Sig and me. He's just a guy who works for my brother, and my neighbor.

"Sig," I say quietly. I'm not sure why I feel the need to be quiet. I step further into the room and peek around the kitchen island. He's not lying on the floor in a pool of blood, so that's a good sign.

Setting the dish of soup on the counter, I move down the long hallway, the floors creaking as I tiptoe toward the one bedroom and bath on this floor. I look down at my feet and can't help admiring the Persian carpet he's got over his refinished hardwood floors. The man has good taste, that's for sure.

He's also very tidy. Leaning into the bathroom, I'm surprised by how clean everything is. There are no towels, pajamas, or undies on the tile like at our house. *What?* Don't judge. I'm busy. Besides, Maddy's spending a few nights at her grandparents' place, so now I've got all the time in the world to clean and do laundry.

Stepping further down the hallway, I see the bedroom door is ajar. Pushing it open slowly, I lean my head in first and see him. He's lying facedown on his king-size bed. His body is at a diagonal on top of all of the covers. I hesitate at the door, because all he's got on are some tight boxers. Adam used to wear those. He called them boxer briefs. No matter; it's obvious Sig Engel can fill out a pair of those damn things. At least by the looks of his ass. I don't need to know about the front. Not at all.

Padding up to the bed, I move around it until I'm up at the top left corner, closest to his head. Leaning down, I whisper, "Sig?"

Without thinking, I run my hand over his forehead. He's hot. Looking down at his tattoo-covered back, I can see his skin is flushed. I lean over and touch him.

"Sig?" I say a little louder.

Still nothing.

Placing my hand on his shoulder, I push on it hard enough to jostle him. "Sig?" I say in my full voice. "Come on, wake up."

Still nothing.

"Sig!" I say louder. Both of my hands are on his shoulders. I'm doing my best to roll him over, but damn, the guy is big. "Sig. Wake up."

When I hear him take in a gulp of air, I feel the tenseness in my own shoulders loosen up. "Sig?" I ask again. "Roll over, hon."

"Babe?" he says hoarsely.

I suppose he's referring to me. But, hell, it could be anyone.

I'm pretty sure he calls all women that name. "Yep. Babe is here. Roll over onto your back."

With a loud groan and the creak of his wooden headboard, Sig Engel rolls over. I do my best to keep my eyes above the boxers, but once or twice I let my eyes flicker over that area. Let me just say this—I suspect he is proportionate. Damn.

Enough of that. This man is sick. I reach over and touch his forehead and cheeks.

"Sig? What have you taken? Did you take anything for the fever?"

He mumbles something, but I can't make it out. "Sig? I need for you to get up. Let's get into the shower to cool you down a little bit."

He grumbles this time.

"I can't lift you, so you're going to have to help me."

"No, babe. I'm fine," he says softly, his eyes never opening.

"Sigmund Engel," I say in my bossiest mom voice. "Get up."

Now he looks at me.

"Up. Up-up-up," I say as I tug on his hand. "Let's get you cooled down."

"Okay," he says softly. With great effort, the big guy pushes up to sitting. I give him a minute to get his bearings.

"Let's go. You're too hot."

"*You're* too hot," he says softly.

"Not as hot as you, Sig."

"Thanks," he says with a smirk.

What the hell? That wasn't meant as a compliment.

I finally get him on his feet, wrapping my arm around his waist. We walk toward his door, out into the hallway, and into his bathroom. A bathroom that has been completely renovated and expanded. His is now twice the size of mine. He must have used the space where I have my washer-dryer closet. Nice.

Once in the bathroom, I reach in and turn the water on. I

want it cool but not cold. When I turn to reach for him, I squeak in surprise. He's naked. Completely. And. Utterly. Naked. I do my best not to seem shocked at the sight, but let me just address something I mentioned earlier. Yes. He's proportionate. Maybe more than...

Growing some lady-balls, I reach for his hand. "Come on, Sig. Get in under the spray." I notice a built-in bench in his massive shower, so I point him in that direction. Once he's seated, I move the spray nozzles—yes, I said *nozzles,* as in more than one—until they're all directed at him. "Stay just like that."

"Sure, babe," Sig says, moving his head up and down slightly. When he winces, he stops moving his head.

"I'll be right back."

I quickly strip his bed of the sheets, tossing them in the nearby hamper. Searching for a fresh set, I locate them on a shelf in his walk-in closet. I peek into the bathroom and see Sig still seated as I left him, so I quickly change his sheets and pillowcases and prepare the bed for him. Back in the bathroom, he hasn't moved. I open the medicine cabinet and pull out cold medicine as well as acetaminophen. Next, I locate a towel hanging on what I guess is a warming rack. It's not turned on, so the towel is just room temp. Poor baby.

"Sig?" I reach in and turn off the shower. "Can you stand up?"

He nods, saying, "Sure."

I hold out his towel; he takes it from me and wraps it around his waist. Without a word, he moves past me, into the bedroom, and flops face first back onto the bed.

"Sig. I changed your sheets."

"Thanks, babe."

"No," I chuckle. "I want you to crawl under them."

"Too hot."

"Damn it, Sig. Do as I say." Okay, I broke out the mom voice again. I can't help it. This isn't easy.

"Okay." He pushes himself up far enough for him to move over to a pillow and slide beneath the sheets, completely naked.

I need to stop thinking about naked Sig Engel.

Moving back into the bathroom, I grab the medicines I found and pour water into a small glass from his counter. "Here," I say, holding out two pills. "Take these."

Sig opens his mouth, and I drop them in like he's a baby bird. I giggle at the thought. "Now drink this."

Lifting his head, he takes the glass and throws back the entire contents. "Drink this." I measure out some of the cold medicine and hold it out. Doing the same as he did with the water, he drinks down the fluid, wincing at the taste.

Looking at the bottle, I wince myself. What would possess the man to buy honey-peach-flavored cold medicine? Yuk.

"You hungry?" I ask softly.

"No." He blinks up at me. A small smile appears on his full lips. "Babe. Adam was right. You really are *tesoro mio*."

I'm stunned. I can't move. Hell, I can't breathe. How? How the hell does he know what Adam used to call me? *Tesoro mio* means "my treasure" in Italian. Nobody knew that. *Nobody*. He only said it when we were alone. Mostly in our bed.

"Fuck!" I shout. "How do you know that?" I screech. "Have you been reading my letters?"

What the ever-loving fuck?

I glare down at him, but he's asleep. Fucking sound asleep. I'm not sure what to do. Part of me wants to shake him awake so he'll talk to me. The other part, the dominant one, wants to stab him with the first sharp object I can find.

When I don't see anything lying about, I turn and march out of his bedroom, down the hallway, past the kitchen, and through the front door. I slam it shut behind me, and I'm out of there. I get across his driveway and onto mine before the tears start to fall. Tears I've been holding for a long, long time.

"*Tesoro mio,*" I say, trying to get into my own home. "*Cuore mio.*" My heart. That's what I said back to him. "Oh, God." I cry harder. I'm still standing on my front porch, because I can't seem to figure out how to open my door. "Fuck." I turn and lean my back on my door and slide down onto my concrete front porch. I'll just stay here for a minute, until I calm down.

CHAPTER SIX

Molly

IT ONLY TOOK HEARING my neighbors talking in their front yard to propel me into my house. I'd stopped crying, mostly, which made it easier for me to open my unlocked front door. I guess my blubbering made me incapable of turning the doorknob. Crying can be cathartic. This time was no exception, since all that sobbing helped me work through what I heard back at Sig's house. I'm positive he hasn't read Adam's letters. They're locked up tight, so that feat is impossible.

Once inside, I sit down in Adam's La-Z-Boy recliner. The thing has seen better days, since he'd bought it several years before we moved in together. He loved the stupid thing. There's this one tiny stain on the arm from me that Adam bitched and moaned about for days. I don't even know what it is. Chocolate? Probably. I do love my chocolate. I run my finger over the stain and smile. I'd give anything to hear him bitch and moan about it, or hell, about anything. I smile thinking about him. The military

29

created a neat-freak husband. It was Maddy's rocker when she was a baby. It was one more connection to her father and even if I have to have the damn thing rebuilt at some point; it will always be there.

I blink thinking about Sig's house. I knew he was in the service, but I didn't put two and two together. He's got the same compulsion—everything in its place. Looking around my house, I scoff. Adam would shit if he saw our house now. Molly's toys are everywhere. I've got laundry spilling out of hampers and elsewhere. I haven't done the dishes in three days, and my bathroom is *dis-gus-ting*. I'd planned to clean while Maddy was at Adam's parents' place. They take her once a month for a few days. It's good for everyone. It gives Maddy time with Adam's family, and it gives me a breather. But now I've got to think about this stuff with Sig. He was too out of it for me to get anything more out of him.

He knew Adam.

That part is clear. But how? Were they in the same unit? I don't recall hearing that name in any of Adam's letters, emails, or Skype calls. Honestly, if Sig was mentioned, it would have been in the letters. That's when he told stories about the other guys in his unit, since we used Skype for, erm, other things. I remember some names, one in particular: Angel. I thought it was a funny name for an Army Ranger, but they all had nicknames. Adam's was Bones, probably because his last name was Barone.

Sighing, I stand up from the rocker and stare at my house. Then I peer out my window at Sig's house. I just left him there. The guy is sick, and I just ran out of there. Well, I *did* give him medicine before I left. I'll go over later—take him some Gatorade or something with lots of electrolytes. Maddy has some kid stuff like that. I'll also need to take him some more soup, since I left his out on the counter. Then, when he's lucid,

I'll ask him some very pointed questions. And the ass had better answer them, or I'll find that sharp object I fantasized about an hour ago.

SEVERAL LOADS OF LAUNDRY LATER, I find myself back on Sig's porch. I don't even bother knocking. I open his screen door, turn the knob, and enter his house. It's dark in the living room, so I search the wall for the switch I know is there. When I find it, I flip on the overhead light. Looking left and right, I note again how tidy his place is.

"Yep. Military."

Stepping into his kitchen, I place the fresh soup in his fridge along with several bottles of Pedia-Aid. The stuff tastes like shit, but it works. Taking a bottle in hand, I walk straight to his bedroom. The second I cross the threshold, I wince. He's naked. I can see that because he's tossed all of his blankets off himself and he's lying at an angle on his bed again. This time, he's on his back. I touch the top of his foot, and it feels hotter than before.

"Sig." I shake his foot. "Sig."

The man doesn't move, which is a worry. I move around the bed and nearly step in what I can only assume is vomit. From the yellow-pink color, I'm going to say it was the cold medicine. "I don't blame you, dude. That stuff was gross."

I scan his body, doing my best to skip his frank and beans. I guess in his case it would be more kielbasa. Ha! See? I've still got a sense of humor. I get myself under control, because now isn't the time. Sig needs help.

Moving up his body, I pause at his tattoos. I haven't really examined them before. I mean, when was I going to do that? It certainly wasn't appropriate when I was spying out my window as he mowed my little lawn shirtless. Right? Or the few times he's been over at Keeton's swimming? I didn't have enough time then, since I was with Maddy and doing mommy stuff. But *now* I've got some. Staring at his pecs, I blink at the set of wings on the right side of his chest. I half expect to read something around those like a date or a name, but there's nothing. There's a large star with the US Army logo on his rib cage. Adam had the same one. On his left pectoral are letters in an arc over his nipple. They don't spell out any words unless you think A.B.A.C. is a word. I don't. But they could represent names. Adam's initials were A.B. but I don't know who A.C. would be. Hell, they could be the first letters of his favorite foods for all I know.

Sig moans, and my attention moves from his ink to his face.

"Sig?" I ask quietly. Leaning a little closer, I place my hand on his cheek. "You're still burning up." I pull the thermometer that I use on Maddy out of my pocket. Swiping the metal plate across his forehead, I wait for the beep and check the temp. "Damn, Sig." It reads 104. He needs medical attention. He's been ill for several days. He shouldn't still be like this. "If you don't wake up for me, Sig, I'm going to have to call an ambulance, because I won't be able to carry your big body out to the car." I sigh, trying one more time. "Sigmund Engel," I say bossily, and I shake his shoulder one last time. Still nothing.

Standing up, I rub my hands over my face, trying to figure out what I should do. I grab my cell phone out of my pocket and call Keeton.

"Speak," he grumbles on the other end of the phone. "It's Friday night. This better be good, Molls."

"I can't get Sig to wake up. I had him up earlier today—gave him some medicine—but now he's moaning, and he won't wake up."

"Shit," Keeton mutters.

"Should I call an ambulance? I'd take him to the emergency room, but I can't carry him to the car by myself."

"Maddy at the grandparents'?"

Keeton knows our routine, and she only has one set of grandparents, since our parents died in a car accident when I was young. "Yeah."

"I'll be there in fifteen. Call Eric. I won't be able to manage that giant either."

I snort into the phone, because I know he could. He just doesn't want to. "I will."

I call Eric next, who answers in pretty much the same way as Keeton. "Be there in ten," he grunts.

I look down at the naked man and decide to put pants on him first. I can't very well let him out of the house naked. Scanning his bedroom, I locate his dresser. I open his top drawer first and see it's filled with personal items. His wallet sits on top. I grab that in case he needs it at the hospital. Below that is a square leather box with a symbol I recognize, a Purple Heart. I'm tempted to open it, but now is not the time to be nosey. I try to push the drawer closed, but it stops halfway.

"Shit." Something must be jammed. I try to pull it back out, but it won't budge that way either. Reaching my hand inside, I wiggle my fingers around until I feel it. Something, some kind of paper, is caught in the drawer slider things. When I get a good grasp of it, I wiggle it loose until it's in my hand. Staring down at it, I nearly choke. It's a photo. Of me when I was in my early twenties. Not only that, the thing is worn nearly to tatters. The edges are all frayed and dirty like it's been handled a lot. Touched. I turn it over and nearly pass out. Placing the photo over my heart, I press both hands to the back of it. A sob escapes me. This was Adam's. I gave it to him when he left for one of his deployments. I remember writing the note on the back like it was yesterday.

Keep this photo with you at all times so you don't forget about me. I'll be here, Adam, waiting for you. Always. All my love, Molly.

Why the fuck does Sig have this?

Sliding the image into my back pocket, I wipe my eyes and swallow back the pain. I need to get Sig better so he can explain all of this. Opening up two more drawers, I finally locate some sweatpants. I'm stepping toward the bed when I hear the front door open and close.

"Where you at, Molls?"

"Bedroom!" I shout. I wait for Eric to enter the room before I attempt to dress the mammoth man on the bed.

"Whoa, that's something I never wanted to see." Eric chuckles. "Dude needs some damn pants."

Holding up the sweats, I say, "Help me get these on him."

Eric nods, "I'll take the feet. I'm not getting any closer to his junk."

I roll my eyes, but I do as he asks. As Eric works the pants over his feet, I move up onto the bed on my knees. When I get to his hips, I stare down, wondering how we're going to do this. Deciding the best way to lever him is to straddle him, I lift my leg over him until my ass is hovering over his chest. Reaching my hands beneath his ass, I say, "I'll try to lift him here if you slide the pants up."

With as much strength as I can muster, I groan as I try to lift his hips. I get them about an inch off the bed. I'm struggling. "Hurry," I say breathlessly. When nothing happens, I look up and see Eric laughing. "Fuck off, Eric. Let's go. The man is sick."

"Right." He clears his throat and pushes the sweats up his

legs and thighs. We work together to get them under his ass and above his junk. By the time we've got him half dressed, Keeton steps into the room.

"What the fuck are you two doing?" Keeton's stern expression is laughable.

"Dressing him," I say, wiping the sweat from my brow. "He's heavy."

"I'm not heavy," Sig mumbles.

I squeak when I feel it. Sig's hand on my left ass cheek. I guess it is right in front of his face. He moves his palm over my bottom gently, whispering, "*Tesoro mio.*"

My body stiffens instantly, and my legs are off him and the bed in less than a second.

"Come on," I sigh. "Let's get him to the ER."

Eric moves around the bed and cusses when he sees the sick.

"Sorry. I didn't get a chance to clean that up."

Eric begins to gag. He's got a weak stomach when it comes to stuff like this. You'd think he'd be better about it since he became a father, but I guess not. Stepping around the bed, I push him away. "You guys grab his arms; I'll hold his shoulders until you get him upright."

On the count of three, we get Sig on his feet. I think we moved too fast, because the next thing we know, Sig is dry heaving.

"Ugh," chokes Eric. He gags again, but by now I'm in front of all three guys. "Come on. Let's go."

The guys wrap their arms around him and lift him far enough off the ground to get him out of his house and to Keeton's car.

"Don't get sick in my ride, man," Keeton warns.

Once we have him buckled in, Eric jumps in his truck. "Meet you at the ER?"

"Yep."

I slide into my SUV, but it won't start. "That's because you need your key fob," I mumble to myself. Stepping out of my car, I race into my house and grab my purse. Before jumping back into my vehicle, I jog over to Sig's to get the wallet I left on his dresser. While I'm there, I quickly clean up the floor in his bedroom. I'll come back and change his sheets and tidy up after we know he's okay. Plus, it'll give me more time to snoop.

I need to know more.

CHAPTER SEVEN

Sig

WHY DO I feel like I've been hit by a truck?

I blink several times, attempting to adjust to the bright lights above me.

Where the hell am I?

There are beeps and whirring noises to my left and the sound of soft snoring to my right. I turn left first and see machines blinking. I'm in the hospital? Turning right, I see blonde hair. She's got her head on my bed, her eyes closed. Molly is fast asleep. I wiggle my fingers, tempted to touch. She's got beautiful hair. It looks so damn soft.

"You're finally awake, huh?" My eyes jerk up as a woman saunters into my room. She's wearing pink medical scrubs. "Hey, handsome," she coos, "How're you feeling?"

I have to think about her question. "Like shit." I'm not kidding. My head aches, as do my muscles. I'm also hungry as hell. "I'm hungry."

"No food for you just yet," says another woman. This one is wearing a white coat over her clothes. She is also holding a clipboard and wearing a stethoscope around her neck.

As the nurse wraps my arm in a blood pressure cuff, I watch as the woman in white pumps hand sanitizer into her palms. As she rubs them together, she makes her way closer to the bed, "Mr. Engel. I'm Dr. Schmidt." She holds out her now disinfected hand to me; I shake it and wince as the cuff tightens around my arm.

Damn, those things hurt.

"Hmm, one thirty over seventy," she says the nurse to Dr. Schmidt.

"Is that bad?" The nurse is making it sound bad.

"Slightly elevated. Not uncommon with the flu."

Okay. Now at least I know why I'm here. I've got the flu.

"You were severely dehydrated as well," adds the doctor.

"How long have I been here?"

"Overnight. Your friends and wife brought you in."

"Friends?" I look down at Molly. "My wife?"

"Yep. Good thing too."

Yes. I look down at her again. *Tesoro mio.*

Before I can say anything else, I feel my eyes droop.

"I just gave you something that will help you sleep."

"Okay." And then I'm out.

I WAKE TO WHISPERING VOICES. Without opening my eyes, I concentrate on the sound of the woman's voice.

"They want him to stay another night."

I open my eyes but only slightly. I want to see who she's talking to. When I finally focus, I see Molly on the phone.

There's silence. I guess the other person is talking.

"I can't stay tonight. Maddy comes home tomorrow night, and I've got so much shit to do at home." Quiet again, she makes those *mm-hmm* kinds of sounds like she's agreeing with whomever is on the phone. "He shouldn't be here alone." She makes a scoffing noise, which tells me whoever she's talking to is pissing her off. "Fine," she snaps. "I'll stay again, but I need you here bright and early tomorrow."

I open my eyes fully and turn my head toward her. She sees movement and starts to smile, but then it stops. "He's awake. I gotta go."

As soon as she ends her call, I say, "I'm good. You don't need to stay. Go home and take care of your shit."

"No." She leans back into her chair, crossing her arms and legs, giving me a very closed-off vibe. "We need to talk."

Uh-oh.

"What about?"

Molly leans over the side of her chair reaching down. Her arm raises. She's holding something.

Shit.

"Why do you have this?"

"You snoopin' at my place, babe?" I need to buy some time.

"I was looking for something to cover your naked ass. I started with the top drawer, saw your wallet and grabbed that. When the drawer wouldn't shut, I reached in and pulled this out." She holds up the picture again. "It was jamming the drawer."

"Oh." I blink a few times, wondering what I should say. I'm stalling.

"You gonna answer me, Sig?"

"Now isn't the time."

"You called me *tesoro mio*."

Fuck.

"Only one other person called me that. Spit it out, Sig. I *need* to know."

She emphasized need. She does need to know. I'm just not sure I can tell her. Not everything, anyway.

"Can I get something to drink? Eat?"

"Stalling?" she arches her brow.

My stomach growls loudly on cue. *Thank you, stomach.*

"Fine." Molly stands, reaching for the nurse call button I didn't know I had.

It beeps for several seconds, then a female voice says, "Yes?"

"Sig is hungry and thirsty." She speaks for me.

"Let me see what he can have." The voice on the speaker ends as Molly sits back in her seat.

"Spill." Molly is back to her closed-off body language—arms and legs crossed.

"Adam and I were in the same unit."

She nods. "You were a Ranger?"

"Medic." I was also trained as a Ranger, a requirement in special operations command. I wait a beat for her to say something, but she remains silent.

"We went through basic together."

"I've never heard of you." Molly's brows are pressed together in concern.

I doubt she ever heard my real name. "My last name, Engel? It's German for angel."

Molly gasps; her hand covers her mouth. "Angel?"

"You remember that name?"

"Yes," she says in a shaky voice. "Adam wrote about you a lot."

"He was my best friend." I feel my eyes burn. "My brother." I shake my head, trying to push the sad away, but all it does is make my head ache.

"But why, Sig?"

"Why what?"

"Over three years. You've lived here for over three years. You work with me, yet you never thought to tell me you were my husband's best friend?" She stands abruptly just as a nurse walks in holding a tray.

We're both silent as she places it on the rolling table by my bed. Pushing it in front of me, she lifts a plastic dome-shaped lid to reveal a bowl of clear broth. There's also some sort of pureed fruit. Applesauce, maybe. Who knows? No matter; I've got no appetite anymore.

"Babe," I start to say.

"Don't 'babe' me. You lied to me for three fucking years, Sig. Why?"

"I had my reasons."

She starts to pace back and forth at the end of my bed. "What fucking reasons?" Stopping at my feet, she faces me. Our eyes connect, and I see her. I know that look. She's mad, yes. But mostly she's sad.

I'm just going to say it. "You weren't ready."

"Ready? For what? My husband dying? Knowing his best friend is living next door to me? Hell, you've been taking care of us...." She blinks at me. Her arms fall to her sides, and her shoulders slump. In the softest voice, she practically breathes, "You're trying to take care of us."

I nod slowly.

"Why?"

"He asked me to."

"When?" It comes out as a squeak. She knows when.

"Molly..."

"No." She steps around the bed until she's standing at my side. "I need to know." I watch her swallow. I can practically see her pulse beating in her throat. "You w-were with him. That day. Weren't you?"

I nod. "I was a medic."

One lone tear slides down her cheek. "I never wanted to know the details. I know it was an IED."

"Yes." I don't know what else to say. It probably wouldn't make her feel any better if I told her it could have been any of us. Or hell, all of us. But it wasn't. It was Adam. Just Adam.

She nods, but says nothing.

"We were on patrol together. Me, Bones, and Pasta."

"Pasta?"

"Carbonara. Anthony Carbonara."

She whispers, "A.C."

"What?"

"On your chest. You have those letters. A.B.A.C. A.B. is Adam?"

"A.C. is for Pasta, who barely survived that day." If you can call what he's doing now living.

"I don't remember a Pasta."

"He was a newbie."

When she says nothing, I look up at her again. She wants to know. "He..."

"Adam?"

"Yes."

God, I don't want to tell her this here. Now. "He... Adam died in my arms."

Her breath catches, and a torrent of tears begin to flow. "You—You were with him?"

"I was."

"Did he..."

"Suffer?" Yes. But I'm not about to tell her that.

Molly's eyes grow round as though that wasn't her question. "Did he?"

"No."

She releases a breath, but she's not done. "What else? Was he able to say anything?"

I nod. I'm not sure I can do this. "He did."

Molly steps closer until her body rests against the guards on my bed; her hands grip the white plastic so hard I can see white knuckles. "What, Sig? What did he say?"

I feel my own eyes start to water. "Babe…"

"Tell me, Sig. Tell me."

I should have told her years ago, but like I said before, she wasn't ready. I rub my hand over my grimy face; I haven't showered for days.

"Sit down, honey."

She presses the button on the bed guard and lets it fall. Lifting her hip, she sits beside me on the bed. I reach out and take her hand. I'm not sure if that's for me or for her.

Her voice is reedy when she announces, "I'm ready."

Here goes nothing.

"I did what I could, but he was mortally wounded." That's all I'm going to say about the extent of his injuries. "I loved him. I did everything I could to save him."

"I know." Molly speaks softly. She squeezes my hand and repeats it. "I know."

"I worked on him." I was frantic. The blood, it was everywhere. "When he knew… he t-told me to stop. That he needed to say something. So I listened."

Molly presses her eyes closed and tears flow out from beneath her lashes.

"His words were about you." *For* you. "He loved you and Maddy more than life itself, and he was sorry."

"Sorry?" she squeaks. She releases a sob so gut-wrenching, I'm not sure I can continue. "Why would he be sorry?" She runs the back of her hand across her eyes. "I'm the one who should be sorry."

"Molly." I pause, ignoring her guilt. We all have it. But in her case, she has nothing to feel guilty about. "He told me to find you."

"F-Find me?"

I nod. "H-he told me he trusted me—to take care of you."

"Sig," she cries. Molly's sobs are painful to hear, but I need to keep going.

I feel helpless, so I do the only thing I can right this second—I lean forward and place my hands on her shoulders, gently urging her into my arms. "I'm sorry I didn't tell you, honey." I rub her back. I place one hand in her hair and let my fingers run through the silky strands as she continues to cry into my hospital gown. "I'm sorry, babe."

Her voice is muffled, but I hear her say, "I know. Me too, Sig."

"I know how hard this is for you to hear." I need to stop for now.

Her head moves up and down beneath my palm as she croaks, "Thank you for trying to save him, Sig."

I don't respond. How can I? I failed. I fucking failed to save the closest thing I had to family in this world.

CHAPTER EIGHT

Molly

I WAKE up wrapped up in a cocoon of warmth and something else. Something comforting. I can't remember the last time I....

I blink, trying to get my bearings. I'm at the hospital. I remember that. The room is dark, and machines are still making soft sounds around me. I push myself up but feel resistance. Looking over my shoulder, I see Sig's hands on either side of my back, and I'm sort of intertwined with the large man in his hospital bed.

How did that happen?

I relax into the bed again before I remember. He knew Adam. Anger hits me instantly. *He knew Adam, and he didn't say one fucking word about it for three fucking years.* I should strangle him. But I can't. Not yet anyway. I need to process this. I need time to work through everything he told me. One hundred bucks says there's more to his story, but I'm not sure I could have handled more just then.

Rotating my body until I'm on my back, I reach out and gently lift the hand that is now on my stomach. Holding it up a few inches, I slide out from under it and place it on his own stomach. Adjusting my clothes that got all wonky in that maneuver, I look for my purse. Spotting it on the floor, I pick it up and move to the door.

"You goin' home, babe?" asks a sleepy-sounding Sig.

"Uh." Yes, I was going to sneak out of here.

"Go home. Get some real sleep. I should get released in the morning. I'll call Keet or Eric to come get me."

"Okay." I'm going to let him do that. I can't guarantee what my state of mind will be by then. "Bye, Sig." I raise my hand and give him a small wave.

"Bye, babe."

I PASSED out the second I got home. Literally. I fell face-first on my bed and slept for hours. By the time I woke up, the day was half gone, and for some reason, I had no energy to clean my house. Hell, I wasn't sure I had energy for my baby girl. So, I did something I hadn't done in three years: I asked Adam's parents if they could keep her another night. I also sent a text to Keeton letting him know I was taking Monday off.

Now that I have some time, I pull all of my blinds down so my house is dark and cool. Next, I crawl into my closet in search of my small safe. Using the key I keep in my jewelry box, I open the safe and pull out the tall stack of letters from Adam. I have most of the letters I sent to him too, but I don't want to read those. There's also the letter that he wrote just in case. I received that when the army sent me his personal belongings. My breath catches. Just saying those two words brings me pain. I've kept all of his things in a wooden box so that Maddy can have them someday. It's all she has left of him.

Sliding onto the middle of my bed, I stare down at the stack that I've secured with a yellow satin ribbon. I thought it was fitting at the time. Pulling out the first letter, I hesitate to open it. I've read it so many times, the edges of the envelope are worn and dirty, but it's been a while since I've read it—or any of them. Leaning back against my headboard, I open the first letter and read.

Babe,

Goddamn, I miss you so much. I've only been gone two weeks, and it's two fucking weeks too long. If it weren't for the guys here, I'd be going ape-shit crazy. We're moving out in three days, so you may not hear from me for a while. I'll keep writing though...

Finished with that letter, I fold it gently and place it back into the envelope. Setting it facedown beside me, I reach for the next. I read half a dozen letters before I see his name. Angel.

Babe,

I miss you. There's word going around that our leave is going to be postponed. There's been a lot of action in this area. I'll keep you posted. But, fuck, I need to see you. I miss you.

Ha! I wrote that already. I guess it should tell you just how much I mean it. The only thing that's keeping me sane is a new guy who got here a week ago. We call him Angel. It doesn't fit the asshole at all. There's nothing angelic about him. He tells the dirtiest fucking jokes I've ever heard, and he's cranky as shit most days. Well, we're all bitchy most days, I guess.

Anyway, he and I have been talking a lot. He's from out east. He's never been to AZ. I told him he should check it out. I need to write to Keeton about him. He's fucking crazy good at working on anything with a motor, and he's just as creative. Maybe he'll visit us sometime and I can talk him into sticking around Page. Hell, he could work at GCM.

I read letter after letter, each with at least one mention of Angel. Like, Angel is hilarious, or Angel's mom died so he went home for a couple of weeks. When Angel's girl broke up with him because she couldn't take the distance, I could tell Adam was upset. He wrote:

Angel's girl dumped him over email. She met another guy. Jesus, who does that shit? The man is over here serving his goddamn country. She knew that going in, right? Wait... you're not going to leave me, right, Molls? I couldn't take it if you couldn't wait for me, honey. You're my world.

I remember this letter like it was yesterday and how quickly I emailed him *and* wrote him a real letter to tell him how much I loved him, promising I'd wait forever for him. He never mentioned it again. I hope my words were enough to convince him. I hope he never doubted my love for him and my absolute commitment to us, no matter how long he was gone. *Or even if he didn't ever come back.* I was still committed.

Wiping away yet another tear that leaked from my eye, I smile a little. I'm so glad he had a friend like Angel—someone who made him laugh, who obviously watched out for him, and who listened to him as he lay dying. I should be grateful for Sig. I *am* grateful, but I'm also pissed. All this time I could have been talking to someone about Adam.

It's then it occurs to me. *He can talk to Maddy about her dad.* Someday she'll want to hear stories about her father—about his time in the army. Sig can recount those tales. Sure, I've got his letters, plus I've printed out every email exchange between the two of us. But hearing those stories firsthand from Adam's best friend will be priceless.

I spend the rest of the day lying in my bed. I read a letter every so often, but I can't seem to muster the energy to move off my bed. As the sun sets, I hear a knock on my front door. My gut tells me it's Sig. My gut also tells me I should just pretend I'm asleep, but I can't do that to him. What if he had a relapse?

Sliding out of my bed, I walk to the front door. Peeking out of one of the three small windows at my eye level, I see him. Well, he's much taller than my little windows, so all I see is his mouth and chin. Opening the door about a foot, I pop my head into the opening. "You okay, Sig?"

He clears his throat. "Yeah. I got home around noon. I took a nap, since you can't get a good night's sleep in the hospital. I woke up worried."

"Worried? About what?"

"You."

"Me? Why?" Oh, wait, I know why. "I'm fine, Sig. I just need time to process everything. I asked Grandma and Grandpa Barone to keep Maddy one more night." Plus, I took tomorrow off to sulk some more, but I'll keep that to myself.

"Because you needed to process?"

"Process, decompress, feel sorry for myself." I shrug as I own up to my day's events.

"I made you sad, babe?" He runs his hand through his near shoulder-length auburn waves. "I knew it was too soon."

"It wasn't," I sort of snap. "You know what?" I pull the door open wide enough for me to step out onto the porch with him. "I wish you'd told me a long time ago, Sig. I could have leaned on you a little. Nobody wants to bring him up. Ever!" I shout. "They think I'm going to lose my shit if Adam's name is even mentioned. Do you know how that makes m-me feel?"

His eyes are on me, intense, unwavering. "No. How?"

"Like they don't remember him. I want Maddy to hear about her dad. And not only from me. Sure, his parents talk about him, but she needs to hear stories from all of us. I know she didn't get to meet him, but that doesn't mean she shouldn't know what an am-amazing person he was." My tears have started up again I'm a blubbering fool. "You know what I mean?" I squeak.

He wraps me in his arms, and I sink into him.

With his lips against the top of my head, he says, "I know what you mean. I miss the hell out of him too. There have been a million times at the shop or at one of your family shindigs that I've wanted to tell you all the things I remember about him. But I never felt like it was my place."

"You loved him like a brother. It *was* your place."

"Okay." He releases a sigh into my hair. His hand moves up and down the center of my back. It soothes me. His big hand is so warm, I can feel it through the cotton of my tee. "Good. Yeah. I'd like that too."

CHAPTER NINE

Sig

WHEN I WAS WALKING OVER, I still felt a little run-down. Once I had her in my arms, BAM, I was cured. This woman is something else. She's so fucking strong, but also soft and real and honest. She's everything Adam always said she was. He knew he was dying that day. He did what any good man would do to ensure his wife and daughter were taken care of, something I didn't tell Molly about earlier and never will.

That fucking hellish day. One I'll never forget. A day that wakes me up in the middle of the night in cold sweats screaming at the top of my lungs. Not because I was wounded. No, because watching my brother die was gut-wrenching.

His words. I'll never forget his words.

"Sig, man. Stop," he said. I was using everything in my unit one pack to stop the bleeding. But it was useless. His

*legs were gone. Blood was everywhere. "Listen to me."
His voice was weaker than before.*

*I couldn't stop though. I had to do what I could to
save him.*

*"Angel," he said, wincing in pain. "Just stop. Listen
to me."*

*When I finally looked at his face, I knew. His face
was unnaturally pale. I'd seen it before. I looked into his
eyes, and I stopped.*

"I'm listening, Bones."

"Love her." His voice is weak, so I lean closer.

I know what he said, but I need to be sure. "Molly?"

*"Go to her. Take care of her. Love her and my little
girl."*

*With the war zone all around us I could barely
hear him.*

"Promise me."

"I promise, man. I'll take care of them."

"Love her. You're..."

I'm losing him. Goddamn.

"You're the only one."

*Fucking hell. Why him? It should have been me. I've
got nothin', nobody.*

*"I will. I promise, man. I'll love her. Both of them.
Almost as much as you do."*

"Thank you, brother."

And then he was gone. My best friend, my brother, was
gone. Dead in my arms.

CHAPTER TEN

Molly

I DON'T KNOW how long Sig and I stand on my front porch hugging each other. It could have been five minutes or an hour. All I know is, it feels good. *Really* good. I also can't help wondering what the hell is going on with me and Sig. I'm feeling things I probably shouldn't. There's no way he'd even think of me like *that*—bro code, after all, So, no, I'm sure he's just being a friend, brotherly.

Ugh, *brotherly*. Don't I have enough brothers?

Slowly pulling my head back, I look up at him. My God, he's gorgeous. His body is amazing too. The hardness of the muscles on his chest are giving me impure thoughts. His hardness feels right against my way-too-soft body. I have no idea where these thoughts are coming from. A couple of hours ago I was on my bed, crying my eyes out, reading my deceased husband's letters, and now I'm thinking about my handsome neighbor in all the wrong ways. Who does that?

Me, it seems.

"You hungry?" I ask the second he looks down at me. Time to change the subject, or at least the subject that's swirling around in my head.

"I am. They didn't feed me at the hospital, and I was too tired to eat when I got home."

"Soup?" I say with an arched brow.

"You cookin'?"

I nod.

"Then whatever you make will be fine."

I pat his hard pectoral with my palm and force myself to leave his arms. It sucks. I'm instantly chilled. "Come on in. I'll cook, you relax on the couch."

"Sounds good, darlin'."

Oh, crap. That's a new one. Darlin'. It gives me a shiver hearing him say that with his deep, raspy voice.

"Let me see what I can scrounge up." I needed to go to the store, but add that to the list of shit I didn't get done this weekend.

"Is Maddy comin' home early tomorrow?" he asks from my living room.

"No. Afternoon."

"She'll like stayin' an extra night, won't she?"

From my kitchen, I yell, "Yeah." The man knows my girl and our schedule as well as we do. I hear the television come to life and don't hear anything else from him. I make us chicken noodle soup. Nothing fancy, from a can, but it's all I have. Grabbing some saltine crackers, I make my way into my living room where Sig is leaning back on my couch, legs spread and arm over the back of the couch. He looks comfortable. At home. What the fuck am I going on about? *At home?*

As I enter the room, Sig stands. "Here," he says, reaching out to me. "Let me help."

"I've got it," I say with a small smile. Bending, I place his bowl and crackers on my old coffee table and pull myself up to full height. "What do you want to drink? I've got water, milk, and some juice."

"Water is fine. Thanks." He gives me a sweet smile. I like it.

"Are crackers okay, or I could make you some toast—"

"Crackers are perfect. Now stop fussin' and let's eat. You can tell me what you feel like watchin'."

Without a word, I walk back to my kitchen. Adding ice to two glasses, I fill each with water. I look around for a tray or something but give up and take the water out to Sig before I get my own bowl of soup.

Once everything is delivered, I sit next to Sig. I reach forward to grab my bowl and realize we're missing an important item.

"Spoons," we say simultaneously.

"Let me," he says, starting to stand.

"I've got it." Jumping back up, I grab two spoons and I'm back on the couch in seconds. "Now," I chuckle. "Let's eat."

Sig hands me the remote.

"Want to watch a movie or are you in the mood for a game?" I ask him.

"Movie," he says between bites, adding, "Mm. Good soup, Molls."

Giggling, I say, "I slaved over it." Pressing a few buttons on the remote, my movie subscription channel appears. "Comedy? Drama? Chick flick?"

With one brow arched, Sig responds, "Comedy."

I choose one that my brothers have always loved. "Good?"

"Great. One of my favorites."

I'm about to ask if he'd rather watch something newer, but I decide not to. We eat our soup and watch the introduction. After a few scenes, I notice Sig is finished with his soup. I pick up the bowls to bring them into the kitchen. Sig reaches out, picking up our now empty water glasses and the remaining crackers. "I'll get it, Sig."

"I'll help."

He follows me into my kitchen. I'm feeling nervous, so I blurt out, "I'd like to take this wall down." I nod to the wall that separates my kitchen and living room. "Was that hard to do?"

"Nah. It's not load bearing. It wasn't bad."

"Who did you hire to do it?" I don't think he hired anyone, but I'm doing my best to make conversation.

"No contractor. I did it."

"Oh."

As I rinse the bowls and prepare them for the dishwasher, I turn and see he's got his hip resting against my counter and his arms are crossed over his chest, making his arms look massive.

Stop it, Molly.

"Your kitchen could use a remodel," he adds, looking around my space.

"Yeah." Adam and I never meant to stay at this place long enough to remodel. He wanted to build on the piece of land we bought. The one that's down the road from Keeton's house. But that was years ago. "We were going to build."

Sig nods. "You were going to build on some land out by Keet, right?"

"That was the plan."

Sig's voice is so soft it's almost a whisper. "You still want to do that?"

I shrug. "I'd like to live out by my brothers, but I don't know."

"I get it. You feel like you're moving on with your plans without him."

My breath catches. I feel my eyes burn. I'm not going to cry though. Instead, I croak, "Yes."

"Darlin'," Sig says, moving closer. "I can tell you with absolute certainty that he'd want you to be out there with your brothers. He'd want you safe and near family. For you and for Maddy."

Shit. Fucking tears.

"Yeah?"

Sig uses his finger to move a strand of hair hanging in front of my eye. "Yeah."

Wiping away a few tears, I laugh. "You just want me gone so you don't have to deal with my shit anymore."

I half expect Sig to laugh and nod right along with me. But that's not what I see. Nope. He's scowling. Really scowling. "If you think that, you haven't been payin' attention, babe."

Sig takes one more step toward me. I feel my breath catch again, but instead of tears threatening, my heartrate doubles. I should step back. I should pretend I've got to finish the dishes. Hell, I should push him away, but I can't. I won't.

His hand moves up my arm, making them tingle. My nipples harden, and I don't remember the last time that has happened with a touch. Years.

"Molly?" Sig whispers. "The last thing I want is for you to move away from me."

My mouth is dry. Speaking isn't going to be easy, so I just say, "Oh?"

"Yeah, oh," he chuckles. "I love bein' your neighbor."

I deflate. Like a balloon in the Arizona heat. He loves being my neighbor. *Just* my neighbor.

"Stop it."

My eyes jerk up to meet his. "Stop what?"

"Stop thinking I mean *only* my neighbor." His thumb runs along my jawline, and it feels good. Erotic. "If I weren't gettin' over this flu shit, I'd kiss the fuck out of you right now, Molly. But I can't risk you catchin' it too."

I can't believe I'm about to say this. "I've had my flu shot."

Sig smiles. And not his normal smirk. No, this one is full-on. Damn, he's got perfect teeth. "All right, darlin'. You sure?"

I feel my head move up and down, but that's because my words are gone. I watch as he lowers his head. He moves so slowly, I'm sure he's trying to give me time to change my mind. But I do the opposite —I push up onto my tiptoes and meet him halfway. When our lips touch, I freeze. I'm not sure I remember what to do next. It's okay, though, because Sig knows. He takes my bottom lip between his two soft ones and suckles on it for a second. His head moves a little, and I feel his tongue sweep across the same lip he was just nibbling on. That's when I remember. Sliding my hands over his shoulders and around his neck, I pull myself up, opening my mouth as I go.

Sig doesn't hesitate after that. His hands wrap around me and down over my ass. He lifts me until I'm sitting on my kitchen counter. I'm still shorter than he is, but it's better. Sig nudges my legs open so he can move in closer. We're pressed so tightly together, there isn't a part of the front of my body that isn't touching him. Not one part. I feel all of him. He's hard, and that part of him is pressed into me at just the right spot.

"Sig," I say, pulling away slightly. I'm panting like a dog in heat.

"Molly," he says back. "You're fucking beautiful."

"You too." I lean in and kiss him hard and fast as I wrap my legs around him, using the backs of my legs and feet to press him closer.

"Jesus, woman." Sig presses his erection into me, thrusting his hips rhythmically.

When he hits me in the exact spot I need, I pull my mouth away from him to moan. "There. Right there, Sig."

"You want to come, darlin'? You want me to make you come?"

"Yes. Fuck!"

I feel his hand slide down past the waistband of my leggings. When his warm fingers touch my skin beneath, he mumbles, "No panties, babe?"

"Uh…" I guess I didn't bother. "No?"

"Fuck." He palms me and begins to move his fingers through me.

I open my legs wider and lean back on my counter as I chase my orgasm.

"So. Fucking. Wet." Sig makes a grunting sound as he presses one finger inside of me; his thumb circles my clit.

"Oh, oh," I squeak. "There. Please. Sig." I'm talking like a damn robot, but I can't help it. With only a few more swirls of his finger, I'm throwing my head back and coming like a rocket. "Wow," I mumble.

I slowly raise my head and make eye contact with Sig. He's breathing just as hard as I am. When he pulls his hand out from my pants, I stare as he brings his fingers to his mouth. Sliding them in slowly, he squeezes his eyes shut like he's just tasted the best dessert in the world. "Fuckin' sweet." When his eyes open just as slowly, they're hooded and seductive. "I want to fuck you so bad, darlin'." I'm about to say yes to that idea when he says, "But not yet."

"Oh."

"You're not ready."

The fuck I'm not.

"I can read you like a book, Molly. And you may think you are, but you're not."

Gathering up what confidence is left, I shrug and sit up straight. I place my palm on his hard chest and push. "Let me down."

"Molly," he hisses. "Don't."

Since he won't let me off the counter, I snap, "What? Don't what?"

"Don't be pissed."

"I'm not."

The fucker chuckles.

He. Chuckles.

Then he moves in until his long, hard erection is pressed into me again. In a deep, sexy, and sort of ominous voice he says, "You're not ready for me."

I scoff. "Whatever, Sig." Crossing my arms over my chest, I know I'm pushing the girls up so what little cleavage I have is showing in my V-neck tee.

"Woman," he growls.

"What?" I flutter my eyelashes at him innocently.

Sig moves in until our mouths are an inch apart. "Darlin'." His voice has softened somewhat. "When I fuck you, you're mine. And not just for the night. You get me?"

I blink a few times, then stare into his eyes. I always thought they were light brown, but they're actually amber with brown swirls.

"Molly. Pay attention."

I smirk but say nothing as I swipe my tongue along his lower lip.

"You're playin' with fucking fire, Molly."

"Why don't you stop talking and prove it."

Sig's head moves up until he's staring at my ceiling, and then those golden eyes are back on mine. "I want to. More than you'll ever know, sweet girl, but now isn't the time."

"Sig."

"Jesus, woman. I just got out of the hospital."

"Oh, my God." I place my hand over my mouth. "I'm so sorry, Sig." Wiggling against him, I try to slide off the counter. I'm embarrassed. How selfish can a person be?

"No," he says in his bossiest voice. "Don't feel bad about that. I started this." He points at himself. "Let's just go watch the movie. All I want to do is sit on your sofa with my arms wrapped around ya. You're the best medicine. Yeah?"

"Yeah. Okay," I say with a nod.

CHAPTER ELEVEN

Molly

MY GOD, what was I thinking? The poor man has been ill for days, and I try to hump him like a dog in heat. Thank God it's dark in my living room or he'd see how red with embarrassment I am.

Just then, he squeezes my shoulder. "I hear you sighin' over there, babe. Stop frettin'."

"I'm sorry." It's all I can think to say.

When his warm lips kiss the side of my forehead, I stiffen, but then I relax. He nudges me closer until my head is on his shoulder. With a whisper, he kisses my head again and says, "This is perfect, just like this."

I'd agree if I didn't feel like a damn horndog.

When his palm runs up and down my arm slowly, it's so soothing, my eyes begin to droop.

WHAT IS THAT?

I wake to something hard against my ass. I'm uncomfortable, for sure, but not in a bad way. Turning my head, I see Sig sound asleep behind me. We're still on my sofa from the night before. I have no idea how we got in this position though, with both of us lying down and me the little spoon, but here we are.

I place my hand on his, the one he's got on my stomach. As gently as possible, I lift it just enough for me to scoot out from under him.

"Where you going?" Sig says in a tired voice.

"Bathroom."

"Come back."

Not in a million years.

Jesus, what was I thinking? The memories of the night before come flooding back. I threw myself at him. His neighbor and coworker. *Ugh. His coworker.*

As I speed-walk to the bathroom, I hear him say, "I know you're thinkin' too much. I can hear it."

How does he know that? He couldn't. "Am not," I shout back down the hall. Once I'm done, I wash my hands and pull the door open to find him leaning against the wall opposite the bathroom door. I step out of his way and do my damnedest to ignore the tent in his sweats.

"My turn," he says, brushing past me.

Gathering up what I need to make coffee, I see Sig from the corner of my eye as he leans on the counter just like he did the night before. It's like déjà vu all over again.

"I'm feeling better," he says in a husky voice.

Scooping coffee into a filter, I mutter, "Oh, yeah? Good. Great. I'm glad." Shit, how many scoops was that? I need four, but I'm pretty sure I just added six. "Fuck." I murmur. Pouring the coffee back into the jar, I start over. When his warm hands slide around my waist, I lose count again, so I pour the coffee grounds back into the jar again. When he presses himself against my back, I squeeze my eyes shut so I can concentrate on how he feels there.

Good.

He feels good.

Preparing to try a third time to make coffee, I jump when his lips touch my neck.

He says softly, "You're beautiful in the morning, Molly," and I nearly melt. His breath tickles, but that's not what's waking up my entire body. It's him.

"Here's how this is gonna go, darlin'."

I hold my breath.

"I'm going home. I'm going to head to my bedroom, strip off my clothes, and wait." He skips a beat. "For you."

I suck in a mouthful of air. God, my heart is going crazy.

"If you want me, you come to me. Yeah?"

"Yeah," I say, all breathless and shit.

"I'll give you thirty minutes. If you don't show, then I'll know you're not ready for me. Fair?"

I nod.

"I need words, sweetness."

"Um, yes." I clear my throat. "That's fair."

CHAPTER TWELVE

Sig

I TOOK A RISK. A big one. But I had to do it. I lay awake last night with the most painful erection known to man, but that didn't matter. For one, there was no way I was going to have her, for the first time or any time, in Adam's bed. Call me superstitious, or maybe it's loyalty. Either way, that bed holds too many memories for her, and there is no way I want to get in the middle of those. Her memories belong to her. No, I knew if we were going to do this thing, it had to happen in *my* bed, in *my* house.

With that decided, I next had to figure out the best way to put the ball in her court, so to speak, because if she tempted me, propositioned me one more time, I wasn't going to say no. I mean, I'm not a goddamn saint. That woman is my weakness.

When I saw her standing in her kitchen in her tight little stretchy pants and her wrinkled tee, I had a decision to make. The one I made was the best one I could. I gave her the choice.

If she wanted me, all of me, she'd have to walk that sweet ass over to my place. She'd have to, essentially, come to me.

Damn, that was hard to do, because Molly in the morning is a sight to behold. Her pretty blonde hair was all messy and sexy. Her makeup from the day before was smudged, and she had those little lines from lying on something wrinkled. In this case, it was my T-shirt. Fuck. I would love to wake up to that every single day of my life.

I look over at my bedside clock and scowl. Twenty-five minutes. That's how long I've been waiting. I mutter, "What the hell were you thinking, Sig?" She's not coming. I scared her. I moved too fast. "Fuck."

Just as I'm about to get up, I hear my front door open. I'm frozen in place. I literally can't move. What will she do? What will she say? Is she just stopping by to tell me it's a no-go? Or is she here for me? Holding my breath, I listen as her flip-flops slap against my hardwood floors. I watch as my bedroom door is pushed open the rest of the way.

"I thought you said you'd be naked."

I see her and nearly have a heart attack. She's here in a tiny dress. I swallow so hard I think my tongue went down my windpipe. "I, uh, I thought it'd scare you."

Molly's hands move up to rest on either side of her curvy hips. "You think a lot of yourself, huh?"

"No, I..." I chuckle nervously. "That's not it."

"I've seen you naked. Apparently, you like to strip down when you're sick."

I blush. I goddamn blush, then I choke a little. "Yeah?"

"Yeah." Her sassy expression as softened.

"You're here."

"I'm here," she says as she takes a tentative step.

"Thanks for cleaning up my room."

Two steps closer. "No problem."

My eyes are trying to take her in. "I appreciate that you took care of me."

She stops right in front of me and smiles. "My pleasure."

Without speaking another word, I place my hands on the bare skin between her knees and her little dress. I watch my own hands run over the top of her skin. "So soft." Flattening my palms over her thigh, I slowly move them beneath the end of her dress. I'd like to look her in the eye, but I'm almost afraid to. What if she looks uncertain? No matter; I do it anyway. My eyes crawl up the pretty flower pattern on her dress, past her waist, stopping for a moment at her breasts. I can make out the shape of her hard nipples, which means she's probably not wearing a bra. Her chest is flushed, and it's rising up and down visibly. When our eyes meet, it's not fear or uncertainty I see. It's lust. "You want this?"

"I do."

Wrapping my hands around to the backs of her thighs, I pull her closer until my face is directly in front of her center, her sweetness. "Take the dress off, Molly."

Her hands are shaking a little as she brings them down to the edge of her dress. As she slowly lifts it, I don't know what I expected, but I guess I didn't expect her to be completely nude underneath. My breath catches the second it's over her head and I can take in all that is my Molly. "Fucking beautiful."

Pulling her closer, I rest my face at her core. I breathe her in, wanting to memorize her scent. I move my hands up over her luscious ass and squeeze.

"Sig."

"You gonna let me have you, darlin'?" I mean that just like it sounds. "I want it all."

"Yes."

Scooting back a little, I bring her with me. "Straddle me."

Molly places first one knee, then the second on either side of my thighs. I run my fingers down over her ass and urge her to sit on my legs until her breasts are in front of me. "So much gorgeous body to love, babe."

I feel her stiffen in my arms, "Uh, did you just call me fat, Sig?"

I'm staring so intently at her flushed pink tits, I almost miss the question. "What? No," I say almost angrily. "You're goddamn perfect."

She makes an adorable snorting sound. "I'm far from perfect."

"You're fucking perfection." Choosing to move forward, I do what I've wanted to do for three years. I lean in and place my nose between her smallish tits. Inhaling, I take in what's left of her perfume. Or was it just her soap? I don't need to figure that out right now. No, now I need to run my face across each breast, letting her feel my stubble and my breath. Next, I swipe the flat part of my tongue over one tight little nipple, extra slow. It must feel good, 'cause Molly moans. I do the same to the other side, but this time I take as much of her small breast into my mouth as I can, and press my hands on her ass to nudge her closer so she's right on top of my rock-hard cock. God, I'm so fucking hard. I need to feel her above me, on me.

When she's centered, I press my pelvis into hers once, twice, three times. Enough to get another moan out of her and for her to move against me too. Sliding my palms up her back and back down to her ass, I sigh at the silkiness of all this gorgeous flesh. I think I could spend days, maybe months, just touching her.

"Sig?" she says with a whimper. "Stop toying with me."

"I'm not toyin', honey. I've wanted to touch you for so long. I'm relishin'."

Her ass is wiggling on top of me. "Well, you can relish later."

"You wet, beautiful?"

"So wet." She sounds a little desperate.

"Let's see." I put my hands under her arms and lift her off me. Laying her on the bed, I move to my feet and stare down at her. I watch, like it's some kind of dream, as she spreads her legs for me. My dick is in bad shape. I feel my balls draw up just from the sight of her opening up to me like the prettiest flower in the garden. At this point it's imperative that I'm naked. I yank off my T-shirt first and slip out of my briefs next. Molly says something, but I can't make it out. I know she saw me naked, but probably not like this. I squeeze the base of my cock, then palm myself up to the head and back down. I'm trying to calm the fucker down, but it isn't easy with Molly on my bed looking like a wet dream. "Open those legs for me. A little wider."

"Sig. Come on. Stop dickin' around."

I chuckle at her use of words. "I haven't even started dickin' around, sweetheart." Leaning forward, I place my nose at her center and down into her crease. I moan the words, "So wet," but I doubt she heard them. Running my tongue through her from back to front, I feel a little woozy, light-headed.

No, I'm not getting sick again. It's probably because I've been waitin' for this moment for three fucking years. Three years I've waited, prepared myself, and now it's finally here and I'm about to lose my shit from one taste. Deciding not to embarrass myself, I move up her body, kissing her stomach, swiping my tongue over her navel and up to her breasts again. I lick and suckle them until I feel her hand in my hair. When she pulls it, hard, I chuckle, "What?"

"Sig. Enough. Fuck. Me. Now."

"Whatever you want, darlin'." Reaching over to my nightstand, I pull out an unopened box of condoms. Pulling one out, I hold it up. "Condom?" Why am I asking? Well, part of me hopes she says we don't need one, whether that's because she's on birth control or not. I'd prefer she wasn't, but that's probably jumping the gun a little.

Reaching out, she takes the square out of my hand and tears it open.

Damn.

Placing it on the head of my dick, she rolls it down my shaft slowly. I'm watching her hand squeeze me just right.

When she's done, Molly lies back on the bed. Holding her arms out like she wants to fold me in her arms. I smile and move over to her, letting her do just that. Looking down, I place myself at her entrance and begin to push in slowly.

CHAPTER THIRTEEN

Molly

OH. My. God.

Sig is slowly pressing himself into me while I hold my breath. It hurts a little. I guess it's been nearly four years since...

Sure, I've used my battery-operated boyfriend every once in a while, but that's nowhere near the size of Sig Engel, because Sig Engel is porn-star sized.

"You okay, Molly?"

I choke out my response. "Yeah. Don't stop."

Sig's practically panting, he's breathing so hard, all while I hold mine. I hold my breath until I know he's all the way in. Once he's seated, Sig places his palm on my cheek. "I've never felt anything like this."

I'm having difficulty speaking, so all I do is nod.

Sig slowly pulls back out of me, not all the way, but almost. I look down at where we're joined together. Honest to God, I have no idea how he fit in there. Sure, Adam was big, but not like this. I stare at us, expecting him to push back in, but he doesn't. Instead, he says, "Am I hurting you?"

I blink when I realize he's talking to me. "No. I'm just fascinated by the sheer size of you."

"We fit together like a glove. A tight glove." That's all he says when he pushes back inside, this time much faster.

"Shit." I roll my head back, which pushes my chest out. Sig must be a mind reader, because the next thing he does is latch on to my right boob. His movements in and out of me increase in speed, forcing me to move with him. When he pushes in, I lift my hips. It's fucking glorious. I should be chasing an orgasm or two, but just Sig filling me up is enough for now.

"Touch your clit, darlin'."

I'm a little disappointed by the change in plan until I reach down and locate my clit. With barely a touch, I'm flying off into the atmosphere. I see stars and fireworks. Okay, well, stars at the very least. I know I've been muttering things about how good it feels.

Sig presses into me and brings his lips to mine in a deep, searing kiss. Pulling his mouth away, he groans, causing his dick to feel even bigger than before as he begins to pulse inside of me.

Wow. Just wow. That was something else.

I'M RESTLESS. Sleeping in someone else's bed is foreign enough for me. Sleeping with Sig is something altogether different. First of all, the man is a blanket hog. I've awoken chilled twice now because he's taken all the blankets and the sheet. I finally give up and decide to put my clothes back on. I was sort of hoping for a second round, but we both fell asleep right after the first time.

After dressing, I slide back into his bed. I can't tell what time it is, but I'm guessing it's two or three in the morning. Too early to be sneaking back to my place. Yeah, that's the excuse I'm going with. I'm still hoping for round two. Lying on my back, I place my arm behind my head and ponder this new arrangement Sig and I just embarked on.

"This could be good," I whisper softly. Having a hookup right next door is sort of ideal. I'm sure Sig would enjoy some action now and then. I've often wondered who he's slept with since he's been here. I know he hasn't had anyone serious. I would have met her by now. And lord knows, the ladies of Page have thrown themselves at the man. I've seen it with my own two eyes. Married or not, some of these local women and a couple of men would sell their souls for a chance at Sig, or one of the other guys at the shop. Now that I've experienced Sig firsthand, I can attest to their good taste.

Rolling onto my side and facing away from him, I chew on my fingernail. His side of the bed moves a little, and then I feel an arm slide over my hip and around me. He pulls me into him until my ass is flush against his semihard dick. I want to giggle, but I can tell he's still out of it. Well, I thought he was.

"So sweet, beautiful," he says sleepily. "Love you so much."

I stiffen in his arms. I can't help it. "Sig..."

"Wanted you for-fucking-ever, darlin'." He releases a sound that's more of a snore than anything. "Wanted you and Maddy. Mine."

My eyes start to go sort of wonky. I'm blinking like crazy and having trouble catching my breath.

Love you so much?

There's no way. Sig can't love me.

Wanted you for-fucking-ever, darlin'.

What? He's wanted me? And Maddy? Did he say 'mine'? What is he talking about?

Doing my best to avoid the inevitable panic attack, I wait a few minutes and slide out from beneath his arm. Looking around his room for anything I may have left behind, I grab my flip-flops and step out into the hallway and practically run to his front door. Opening it as quietly as possible, I slip out and slide into my shoes. I'm in my own living room in seconds. Once there, I let the panic attack do its worst. Because what the fuck was all that back there?

I shake my head. "He must have been talking in his sleep. He didn't mean it." Because if he did...

It doesn't matter if he meant it or not. There's only one man I can love and even though he's not here anymore, I know he's watching, keeping an eye on me and Maddy, and while he'll probably give me a pass on the sex earlier, there's no fucking way he'd ever approve of Sig Engel and me. *Ever*.

CHAPTER FOURTEEN

Sig

I KNEW something was wrong the second I opened my eyes this morning. First off, the only person in my bed was me, which means she snuck out while I slept. Now, that could mean one of two things. One, she could have left her oven on, so she ran home to save her house, or two, she freaked out. My money is on number two.

Running my palms over my tired face, I lie flat on my back, staring up at the ceiling. I need to get my ass up and get to work. I've missed a week due to the flu, and I'm sure there's a backlog of work to be done. Now that I have my energy back, mostly, I should be able to knock some shit off my to-do list today. That is, if I can focus on my job and not on the fiery little blonde in the adjacent office.

Rolling out of bed, I walk, still naked, into my bathroom. I quickly shower, shave, and dress. I make a cup of coffee in my single-serve coffee maker and dump a shit-ton of sugar into that.

(A bad habit, but it can't be helped at this point in my life.) Sliding into my work boots that I always dump by the front door, I'm out on my porch in record time. The first place my eyes go is over to Molly's place. Her car is still parked out front, which isn't surprising. It's still early. Ordinarily, she gets to work around eight every morning because she's dealing with Maddy. Since she's still at her grandparents', who knows what time she'll get here?

I stare at her front door and contemplate knocking on it to get a read on her, but she may still be asleep. Besides, I'm not prepared for whatever shit she's going to spew when I do finally see her. Because I *know* Molly Barone. I've watched her in action, and I've seen how her mind works. So, yeah, she didn't leave the oven on last night. Nope. This shit she's about to pull with me all relates to guilt and confusion—mostly guilt. I'd bet my left nut that she thinks Adam would be pissed or that he wouldn't approve of me and Molly. That couldn't be further from the truth. The only problem is, how do I convince her of that fact?

Stepping down off my porch, I make my way to my bike. Shit, I've missed riding my Harley. A week in bed makes you miss the everyday shit. Approaching my badass Harley Dyna Wide Glide, I smile down at her. The bike was my dad's. He left it to me in his will, which shocked the shit out of me. Dad and I didn't always see eye to eye, but I loved the fucker, and I'm pretty sure he loved me. He must've, because he left me his most prized possession. The bike is the shit too. It's even got those classic red flames shooting up the gas tank. Plus, it's a beast of a bike, which is perfect for me since I'm built just like my old man; it's just the right size for me.

Throwing my leg up over the bike, I start it up and feel the rumble and purr between my legs. My dick notices, which reminds me of last night when I was deep inside my woman.

"Shit," I mumble. Running my hand through my hair, I shake my head. "Get it together, man."

Pushing the bike off the stand, I use my legs to roll it backwards. Turning the handlebars, I accelerate until I'm on the street. Once there, I open up the throttle and fly down the road. My body comes alive. There's nothin' like the feeling of being on my Harley, wind in my hair, out on the open road, to make me feel alive. Being on my bike is the next best thing to having sex with my woman. Playin' with my woman's kid in the front yard on a sunny afternoon is also better than riding my Harley. But that's it. Everything else comes after this.

STEPPIN' foot into Gustafson's after being gone so long feels strange. But, the second the guys see me, they all start yellin' shit like, "You're finally fuckin' back," and "Jesus, we thought you died." Yeah, the guys I work with are dicks. But I love 'em, so that's okay.

After a few pats on my back, I make my way into the showroom. Keeton Gustafson is working at his drawing table. "Hey, Keet."

In a gruff voice, he mutters, "'Bout time, man."

"Yeah, sorry."

We both chuckle as he turns around, holding his hand out for a shake. "Glad you're back. Feeling better?" Keeton asks, looking concerned.

I nod and say, "Much." I move closer and look over his back. "Whoa." Keeton's drawn out a new design for one of his custom bikes. "What the fuck is that?" I lean closer. "Steampunk?" I don't know a lot about steampunk, but I know it's cool as fuck with all these mechanical, sci fi, and futuristic elements. The kind of stuff I've seen before always reminds me of the internal working of old clocks or machines. Peering over Keeton's shoulders, I see he's used some of those same shapes on the tank design, as well as on the handlebars, fender, and the leather seat design. "That's cool, Keet."

"Thanks. We got a commission from a writer who specializes in that kind of writing."

"He famous?"

Keeton shrugs. "Must be."

I step to the side of his drawing table. "Can't wait to see it when it's done." And I can't. The guy is fucking talented.

"Me too." Keeton chuckles. "You gonna help me today or what?"

"Hopefully. I don't know what I'm behind on. I'll do my best." Patting him on the shoulder, I walk back out to the shop. I've got two stations, one on the maintenance side of the shop and one over on the custom side. Since I'm good at the electronics side of things, I'm called upon to help out when a bike comes in that's got a fucked-up computer. My favorite work, though, is on the custom side of the shop. There I get to be as creative as I want, plus I get to learn from the best. Not to mention, Keeton's a stellar boss. Who wouldn't want to work for the man? Adam told me I'd be a fool to pass up the chance to meet and work for Keeton. He had so much respect for the man, and now I know why.

As I walk to my workstation on the maintenance side of the store, I smile and wave at some of the guys. There's not one of these men that I wouldn't call a friend.

"Glad you're back," Billy says, holding up his fist. Billy's been here since the day Keeton started.

I fist bump him as I pass. "Me too, man."

Nearly at my station, I see Eric Gustafson kneeling in front of a vintage Indian. "Hey, Eric," I say as I get closer.

"Fuck, Sig." Eric grunts as he stands. "'Bout time."

Holding his hand out, I shake it. "Yeah, it's been a while."

"Glad you're back. Feeling better?"

"Yep." I'm nearly a hundred percent, but they don't need to know percentages.

With a weird smirk and one of his eyebrows arched, he asks, "My sister take good care of you?"

Oh, boy. That's a loaded question, because *did she ever.* "Uh, yeah."

"I bet," Eric says with a chuckle. He turns to reach for something in his rolling tool box. "You two didn't kill each other, did ya?"

"No." Far from it.

"So, you got along?

"Yeah." *What the fuck?*

"You too had some time alone, right? Maddy's been at Adam's parents' place, yeah?"

"Yes." I'm so confused right now. What's he goin' on about?

"Did you finally tell her?"

I stare at one of my best friends and blink. I know my mouth is open a little bit, because I'm surprised by the question. "Tell her what?"

Eric throws his head back and laughs. "Fuck, dude. What do you think I'm talkin' about, dumbass? Did you tell her you love her?"

I'm literally struck dumb. I'm opening and closing my mouth like an ugly-ass carp. "How..."

"How? Shit, *everybody* knows."

"*Everybody?* How?"

"Good. Glad you're not trying to deny it. Playing like you don't know what I'm talking about doesn't suit you."

"Eric. How?" How the fuck does everybody know how I feel about Molly?

"Well, I knew it a few years ago when I overheard you and

Molly bickering like you do every fucking day. When you turned away from her, you muttered somethin' about Molly being yours. As for everyone else? I'd guess it has something to do with the fact that the second Molly's name is mentioned or she walks through the shop or into a room, you stand up about five inches taller, suck in your gut—"

"Hey." I hold my palm over my flat stomach. "I don't have a fucking gut."

"Whatever, Kim K."

"Kim K?"

"Kardashidian or whatever the fuck her name is. They're all vain. Don't get all Kim K about your gut." Eric scratches his arm and continues, "Anyhoo, you get all fuckin' puffed up when she's around and your eyes never leave her. The same thing happens when Maddy's around. I have to say, it's goddamn adorable."

I growl at the insult. "Adorable? I'm not fucking adorable, asshole."

"You are when it comes to my sister and my niece." Eric takes one step closer. Placing his hand on my shoulder, he says quietly, "There's nobody better for her, man. You have my blessing." He turns to get back to work but adds, "But good luck. She can be a handful."

No shit.

I'm not sure what to say. I certainly can't acknowledge any of this right now. Not without talking to Molly first, because Eric's right, she's a handful. Spitfire is probably a better descriptor for her, though. Yeah, if she found out I talked to her brother about us before I talked to her, she'd have my balls on a platter. The thought makes me laugh for some reason. Maybe I am still sick.

"Whatever, dude." I slap him extra hard on the back, and

the pussy makes a squeaking sound. "I need to get some shit done." I step away from him. "Later."

"You can run, but you can't hide," Eric says, laughing. "You're going to have to come clean sooner or later. You'd best do it before she finally starts dating again."

I stop dead in my tracks. I feel my face tighten, and my gaze becomes steely. I look back at Eric. "Over my fucking dead body."

"Ha!" he says with a laugh. "I knew it!"

"Fuck you," I mutter as I stomp angrily off further into the shop. "Molly dating?" I hiss to myself. I repeat what I said a minute ago. "Over my fucking dead body."

CHAPTER FIFTEEN

Molly

I'M NOT SURE WHY, but I take extra time getting ready this morning. Instead of throwing on the cleanest pair of jeans I own and a GCM tee, I opt for a pair of black skinny jeans and a pretty, flowy top that my best friend and big brother's ex-wife, Deb, talked me into. Not only that, but I took the time to blow-dry and flat-iron my hair as well as dabbing a little makeup on my pale face.

Hey. It's not like I don't ever dress up when I go to work. Okay, I don't, not usually, but since every piece of my daily wardrobe is still sitting in laundry baskets, I had to improvise. At least, that's the excuse I'm going with. Because it certainly has nothing to do with the orgasms I had last night or the man who gave them to me. No way. In conclusion, the reason I'm dressing up more than usual is because I only had time to do Maddy's laundry, so my regular clothes are still dirty, and this is all that was left. Period.

Dressed and ready to go, I make coffee to take with me. While that brews, I give Adam's mom, Carmen, a call.

"Hello?" she says in her signature soft voice.

"Hi, Carmen. How's everything?"

"Good. We've had a good time this weekend; she's probably had too many sweets, but that's a grandmother's prerogative, to spoil their grandchildren. Am I right?" She chuckles. "But she misses you."

I feel my nose burn and my eyes water at Carmen's words. "I miss her too." So much.

"Is it okay if we drop her at the shop a little early today? Mike's got a doctor appointment."

"Sure." I pause. "Is Mike okay?"

"Of course, my dear. Just a checkup. But Maddy won't enjoy spending the afternoon in a waiting room." She giggles. "Although I'd love the company."

"I know you would." I honestly hit the jackpot when it comes to in-laws. They have been so strong through all of this, even though their hearts broke right along with mine when Adam died. They were there with me when Maddy was born. They celebrated and mourned with grace and kindness, and I'll always be grateful to them. "I love you, Mom."

"Oh, honey," she coos. "I love you too."

I hang up the phone and close my eyes, trying to get myself together. I always get a little mopey when Maddy's gone, and having her away for an extra day is only adding to that. Plus I feel guilty about last night. While I know I didn't cheat on Adam, it still feels that way.

"Maybe I should get involved with my therapy group again," I say to the cupboard in front of me. I remember them talking about this in group—moving on without our people. I don't recall everything that was said, because the notion of moving on was never a possibility, at least not to me, not then, anyway. But, now? Well, now... I don't know.

With my coffee ready to go, I grab my purse and head out to my car. In no time, I'm in front of my brother's custom motorcycle business. I park in the back, as usual, and sit in my seat for a few minutes. He's here. I saw his bike in its usual spot. I mean, why wouldn't he be here? He's not sick anymore. Nope. He's *all* better.

Leaning over, I peek at myself in the rearview mirror. I fix a smudge of lipstick that's on the right side of my lips. Using what little courage I've got this morning, I open my door and walk in the back door of the shop. Passing Keeton's office, I see his light is off. I check Lainie's office, but her light is off too. She must be home today. Lainie works part-time for Keeton answering phones and doing other jobs, but she mostly works mornings. She uses her afternoons for writing. But today she must be off.

Flipping the light switch on in my office, I wince at the piles of papers and file folders on my desk. My brothers learned a long time ago not to attempt to put anything in my filing cabinets or to pay any invoices after the mess they created while I was on maternity leave. It took me weeks to reorganize my shit, even though Lainie was here part of that time. I think she kept it from becoming beyond repair.

Flopping down in my seat, I glance at the phone. It's blinking frantically, which means there are messages waiting for me—messages that can wait until I sort through the mess on my desk. Nothing happens until I'm able to work in a tidy space.

"Ha." I laugh. "I wish I felt the same way about my house."

"Feel what way about your house?" says a deep voice at my door.

I look up and see Sig leaning against my doorframe.

I stare at him because I have no idea what to say.

He helps me out. "I saw you pull in."

"Yep. Just got here." I point to my desk. "Got a lot to do," I say, while really thinking, *Please take the hint. Please take the hint and leave.*

"I see that. I had a similar mess waiting for me."

Without making eye contact, I pretend to look through the stack of papers on my desk while muttering, "I bet." A jeans-clad leg approaches the side of my desk. With a sigh, I look up until our eyes meet. "I really have a lot to do."

"You left."

I know what he means, but I choose to play dumb. "Left?"

Sig rolls his eyes, and it makes me want to laugh, but I don't, because he doesn't appear to be in a laughing mood. Case in point, he places both hands on my desk, putting his face just inches from mine, and in a low, scratchy voice, he says, "You left me. In bed. Alone."

See?

I stare into his yellow irises and feel my cheeks flush and heat. I know I should tell him the truth, but he's a tad intimidating.

"I thought I left the stove on." Shit. That's a lame-ass excuse.

"Oh, yeah, what'd you cook?"

Good one. The guy knows what he's doing. "Nothing. I was about to when you showed up at my place."

"You were about to cook?"

"Yep."

"Really." It's not a question.

"Really." I release a sigh of relief. "Now, if you'll excuse me, I—" Before I can utter another word, I'm being pulled out of my chair like I'm some ragdoll. He's got my ass on top of my desk on the now-crumpled pile of papers and his mouth on mine even before I can protest.

My God, the man can kiss.

His tongue sweeps into my mouth like he owns the place. I

lean into him and touch my tongue to his. My arms go around his neck and like they can't stand to be left out, my legs do the same around his hips. Sig takes the hint and moves in until we're pressed together. One of his big hands goes into my hair while the other one grabs my ass roughly. He growls into my mouth, and I feel myself become instantly wet.

I'm lost in it until I hear the clomp of footsteps coming from the hallway. Quickly pulling away from him, I squeeze between Sig and the desk, and I'm back in my chair lickity split. The second I'm in place, Keeton steps in front of my open door. "Hey, Molls." I must look like a crazy person, because he adds, "You okay?"

"Sure. Yeah. Just going to kill you assholes for this mess on my desk," I snap. Being bitchy is the best way to get rid of him for now.

"On that note," Keeton laughs, "I'll be in my office." His hand taps the wooden doorframe "I'd get out of there if I were you, Sig. She seems a little testy this morning."

"You're right," Sig says as he starts to head out the door. He turns his head, and our eyes meet again. With an ominous tone, he adds, "But I'll be back."

I DIDN'T LET that happen—I didn't stick around long enough for him to return to the scene of the kiss. Instead, I took care of the slew of phone messages and organized the papers on my desk, then I gave some lame excuse to Keeton about having to pick up Maddy and I was out of there. I don't have my shit together enough to deal with Sig and his alpha bullshit; not to mention the sheer quantity of testosterone in the place was making me dizzy. No. I needed girl time. The first girl I needed was my baby girl. So, instead of having them drop Maddy off, I decided to pick her up early from Carmen and Mike's and drive straight over to see my second girl, Deb.

Pulling into the parking lot of her custom car restoration business called PAR: ProZone Auto Restoration, I look over to my right at GCM. Deb built her building right next door to Keeton's shop. There's no conflict, since Deb works with cars and Keeton only designs motorcycles. They have collaborated on a job or two but, for the most part, Deb's thing is restoring classic cars to better than their glory days. She's good. *Really* good. And successful. Successful enough for two shops. One here in Page, and her original store in Flagstaff, both thriving.

Holding Madalyn, I step up to Deb's open office door.

"Deb," shouts my little girl.

Startled, Deb throws her arms in the air and slaps a smile on her face. "Wow. It's the Barone girls. To what do I owe this surprise visit?" Deb says, taking Maddy from my arms, giving her lots of hugs and kisses.

"I..." I look at Maddy, then back at Deb. How do I talk about this in front of my very precocious three-year-old? *I've got it.* "I need to talk." I look at Maddy again, trying to figure out the right words. "I, erm, had a slumber party last night."

"A slumber party?" asks a perplexed-looking Deb.

"Me too," says my daughter. "Wif Gamma and Gampa."

Running my palm over her pretty little head, I coo, "I know, boo."

Meanwhile, I watch Deb's face morph from a smile to a frown and back to a smile. But not just any smile. No, I see all of her teeth in this one.

Being *the* best friend a girl could ask for, Deb carries Maddy over to her desk. "Maddy? You want to color?"

"*Yes*," Maddy shouts. "I wuv colowing."

I watch as Deb pulls out a stack of white printer paper and a plastic cup filled with permanent markers.

"Ooh, permanent markers?"

Deb turns her head quickly, scowling at me. "You want to talk about this or not?"

"Okay, sure. Yeah." I nod. I need to talk to her, and distracting Maddy is key to making that happen. Once she's settled in, Deb takes my hand and leads me over to the two office chairs she's got against the far wall in her one-hundred-square-foot office.

As soon as she sits, she grabs my hand and begins to speak quietly. "Who?" she asks excitedly. "I mean, I have some theories, but I don't want to say something, so I've gotta ask. Stranger or friend?"

"Friend?" I guess you could say he was my friend. Or at least he was before last night.

Deb squeals and claps like a game show hostess. It's not a good look for my auto mechanic friend. "He finally did it."

"He? Who?"

With a husky whisper, she says, "S-i-g." She spells it out so Maddy can't hear his name and get all interested in our conversation. She adores Sig. "He finally pulled his head out of his ass and made his move. Right?"

How the hell...? "I don't know what you're talking about."

"Of course you don't." She rolls her eyes. "You've been focused on your baby and getting through, as you should. I don't doubt that you missed the signs."

"Signs?" I squeak. "There were no signs."

"So, let's clarify. It was S-i-g, yeah?"

"Yes," I hiss. "What the hell are you going on about? He..."

"Is in love with you."

That's what he said last night, but I'm not going to admit that right now. "No. He's. Not."

"Yes. He. Is. Everybody knows. Well," she chortles, "everyone but you."

"Deb."

She scoots closer, taking both of my hands in hers. "It's time."

"Time?"

"It's time for you to move... forward."

Move on. That's what she meant to say, but she was using less painful words. "Deb."

"You can't tell me Adam would want you to be alone."

"I don't know what Adam would want, because he's dead, Deb," I snap.

"Honey." Deb pulls me into a hug. "You know what I mean. I loved Adam. He was a kick-ass husband, friend, and he would have been an amazing father, but he isn't here. Do you think, for one fucking second, he'd want you to do this alone?"

No. "I don't know. I have my brothers. And you."

"Yes, you do. And your brothers have their own families, so they aren't around as much. You've always got me."

"You're going to have your own family too," I say, placing my hand on her still flat stomach. "When are you and Rob going to announce it?"

"Next weekend. It'll be ten weeks."

"It's safe to share then, right?"

"That's what they say." She smiles.

"How's Rob doing?"

Deb gives me the same toothy grin as before. "Good." Looking me in the eye, her smile lessens, but it's still there. "I've never felt this way before. I loved your brother, but it's not the same. Keet and I were too much alike. Rob's the best man I've ever known. I can't believe, at my age, I met a man who gets me like Rob does. Who has accepted me, a glorified mechanic, just as I am. He supports my work—hell, he hangs out with me while I work on cars."

Squeezing her hand, I say, "I know. He's been such a wonderful father to his girls."

"He has. They've accepted me into their fold with open arms. I half expected one or two of them to throttle me when they found out Rob and I were together. Their mom, Rachel, meant everything to them."

"They're sweet girls, even Keely." I chuckle.

"She's something else, huh?"

"She is."

"So." Deb leans closer. "Are you going to give Sig a chance?"

"It feels so wrong. Like I'm cheating."

"I know. But you're not. If Adam could have met Sig, he'd have—"

"Oh," I squeak. "I forgot to tell you. He *did* know Sig. They were Rangers in the same unit."

"No," she says, sounding shocked.

"Sig is Angel."

"Angel?"

"Adam wrote about him all the time. Engel is Angel in German."

"Mama?"

We both turn to look at my daughter. My daughter, who is now a human abstract work of art thanks to the permanent marker she's got all over her face, forearms, and upper chest.

Deb starts to snicker next to me.

"I'm going to kill you, Deb."

She shrugs. "She's an artist. It's in her blood."

"Fuck," I mutter softly. Standing up from my chair, I quickly march over to the desk and with my best mommy voice, I snap, "Put the markers down, Maddy."

"But, Mama, I'm colowing."

"You're done coloring."

I watch as her chin starts to quiver and her eyes double in size while welling up with tears. "I made you a picthure."

I look down at the drawing of a tall stick person with yellow hair next to a shorter one. Behind us, a much taller stick figure, a house, and a dog. "Is that Daddy?" I point to the largest stick person.

"No," she giggles. "That's Thig."

"Oh, shit," mutters Deb from behind me.

Oh, shit is right. "We don't have a dog." It's the only response I could come up with.

"Not yet," Maddy says softly.

Deb snickers as she says, "Double shit."

Yeah, double shit. "Let's go. You need a bath. If you don't give me grief, I'll make you chicken nuggets." Fuck, do we have chicken nuggets? I didn't get to the damn store.

"Yay!" Maddy shouts. "Chick nugs."

"Yeah, chick nugs."

Straightening up Deb's desk, I peer down at a cashier's check that looks pretty important. It's covered in permanent marker. So much so, you can't make out any of the important information. Holding it up to Deb, it's my turn to smirk. "Look. She made you a picture too."

"Fuck," Deb hisses. "I needed that."

I shrug. "She's an artist. It's in her blood."

"Fuck you," Deb says with a laugh. "Call me later. I want the rest of that story. Then I'm going to convince you it's time to give S-i-g a shot."

"Thig?" Maddy says, looking confused.

Arching my brow at Deb, I turn to leave. "She's smarter than all of us."

With a sigh, Deb grumbles, "I know."

CHAPTER SIXTEEN

Sig

SHE SNUCK OUT. The minute I had a break, I moseyed on into her office, but her light was off. I stepped in front of Keeton's office. He was busy working on his computer, no doubt doing something related to a bike design. "Hey, Keet. You seen Molly?"

Keeton stops clicking around on his mouse but doesn't look over at me. "What's going on with you two?"

It's really none of his damn business. "Nothin'."

"Uh-huh." He finally swivels his seat around to face me. "You finally makin' your move, brother?"

Brother. I know he doesn't throw that word around. He means it like it sounds.

Shrugging, I say, "More or less."

Keeton's cheeks puff out, then he releases the air slowly. "This is gonna be a shit-storm."

"What?"

"You and Molly."

I'm gettin' a little pissed off now about all of the Gustafson grief I've gotten today. In an attempt to keep myself from screaming, I grind out, "How so?"

"Well, first off, I'm not sure she's ready."

My eyebrows move up into my hairline as I wait to hear what else he's got to say.

"Not to mention that you both have fucking tempers."

Nodding, I cross my arms over my chest, doing my best to keep that *temper* at bay. "Is there more?" I say it with gritted teeth. I'm sure he noticed.

"See?" He points at me. "That's what I'm talking about. You're pissed."

"Just say your goddamn piece, man." Fuck.

Moving around his desk, Keeton steps in front of me. "Look, man. You know how I feel about you, hell, how we all feel about you. It's just..."

"What?" I snap.

"Adam was..."

He doesn't know about me and Adam. Lifting my shirt above my pec, I point to my chest to the tattoo of the four letters. "I knew Adam. These are his initials. I was with him when he died, man. He was my best goddamn friend."

Keeton's eyes look as big as saucers. I never really understood that expression until right this minute.

"You what?" Now Keeton sounds pissed. Great.

"I'm Angel. I know he told you about me. About me coming to work for you after we were out."

"Angel?" He blinks several times. His mouth opens and closes until he asks, "As in, Angel from basic?"

My head moves up and down slowly, affirming his question.

"Does Molly know? Because, fuck, if she doesn't, good luck."

"She knows. I just told her."

"And she's still speaking to you?"

"Jesus, man, she wasn't ready before."

"All this fucking time, and you never once mentioned that you knew him? That's fucked-up." Keeton stomps back around his desk and flops back into his chair. "That's fucking fucked-up," he adds, angrier than I've ever seen him. "Why?"

"None of your business." It's not. It's none of his damn business. "That's between me and Adam." And me and Molly now.

His voice has quieted. "Between you and Adam?"

"I... I promised him."

Keeton stares at me. I stare right back. I'm not sure how long we do that.

"You said you were with him?" Keeton's voice is a whisper.

Placing my hands in the front pockets of my jeans, I look down at the ground. "Yeah."

Silence. It's deafening, just like the cliché.

"He asked you to take care of her, didn't he?"

I feel my chin quiver, my eyes burn. Swallowing down the emotion as best I can, I step up to his desk. "He never stopped talking about her or the baby. Or you guys, for that matter, but mostly about Molly. I probably know more about her than you do." I laugh, but it's hollow. "That day..." I look up at his industrial ceiling, then back down. "That day... before he died, he told me to come here. To take care of her and Maddy."

Keeton's nodding, but I'm not sure he realizes he's doing it.

"He told me to l-love her." And then it happens. I cry like a little bitch. "Sorry," I croak. "Been holding that shit in for three fucking years."

Keeton stands and moves around his desk. Pulling me into a hug, he slaps my back, then steps away. "And do you?"

Wiping away the tears from my cheek, I ask, "Do I what?"

"Love her?"

"I do. Like she's always been mine. She's my fucking heart, Keet—her and Maddy."

"Well, fuck," he mutters. "You're crazy."

"Yeah. I know."

"You're sure?"

Why do I need to keep saying it? "I'm sure."

"Because..."

"Look." I run my fingers through my mop of hair. I need a cut. "When you met Lainie and it was all whirlwind and shit..." I pause, trying to find the right way to say this. "Did people tell you not to? That you were goin' too fast? That you were *crazy*?"

A smirk appears on Keet's face. Not surprising, since I already know the answer. "Fuck, no."

"Then stay the fuck out of this."

With a nod and a wave, Keeton turns around and starts clicking again. I'm about to step out of his office when I hear a chuckle. "May the force be with you, man. She's not gonna be easy."

Well aware.

HER CAR'S in her driveway. She's got lights on in her living room, and there's a glow upstairs. She's home. I've given her hours to get her shit together. I haven't been home since this morning. After work, we had a poker night at Ian and Agatha Burke's place. Patting my back pocket, I smile, knowing I'm a hundred bucks richer than I was when I walked into their place. It's funny, really. Nick, a Page cop, and Ian, former FBI, both have obvious tells when we play poker. I should probably tell them, but it's too much damn fun extracting money from them.

Walking across her driveway, I stomp up her front steps and knock. I lean my ear up to the door, listening for something:

footsteps, voices. When I hear nothing, I knock again. I contemplate hitting the bell, but I don't want to wake Maddy. It's only a bit after nine, but she goes to bed early. Frustrated, I knock again, a little harder this time. When the door finally opens, it's only a crack––enough to see one eye, part of her nose, and one half of that plump little mouth.

"Babe," I say, leaning up against the doorframe.

"Sig."

"You gonna let me in?"

Her eye blinks, and she bites the half of her mouth I can see. "No."

I'm taken aback. "No?"

She blows out a raspberry sound, and her lips vibrate. "Sig." Blink. "If I let you in, we both know what's going to happen."

Fuck, I hope so. "Not necessarily."

Her single brow arches. "Not necessarily? Ha."

"I'm serious. If you don't want my hands touchin' all that soft skin, or to have my cock sunk so deep inside that hot, wet, pu—"

"Sig!" she shouts. "Stop." Then she giggles. "You're so dirty."

Shit, I've turned myself the fuck on. My cock has come to life thinking about that sweet pussy. When I speak, my voice feels deeper. Rougher. "For you. I'm dirty for you."

"I need..." Her head moves until her forehead is leaning on the edge of the door. "Time."

I'm choosin' to ignore that for now. "I told Keeton."

"You told him what?" she snaps. The door opens wider, so now I get a glimpse of all of her face and half her lush body. She's wearing short fucking shorts and a tank. No bra. I'm staring at her tits so intently I see her nipples poking out beneath her shirt. Fuck, this woman is sin.

Doing my best to keep my shit together, I answer her.

"About me and Adam." And some other shit that she apparently doesn't like the sound of, since she practically bit my head off just then.

"Oh."

"He was pissed."

"Not surprising."

No, not surprising. Without another thought, I reach out, gently grasping her upper arm. I pull her toward me. The second she's close enough, I step into her, wrapping her up in my arms, and I kiss the shit out of her. There's no messin' around this time. My tongue is deep into her mouth before I've given her a chance to think about it.

"Sig," she says in a sexy voice. "God."

Reaching down, I grip her ass and lift her until she's directly over my cock. "Gonna fuck you against this door, Molly."

"Okay."

Stepping into her place, I kick the door shut with my booted foot. Pressing her back against the door, I slide my hand down until I find a way in. "You're soaking wet."

"I know."

Running my finger through her wetness, I plunge my middle finger into her over and over again. "I want my cock right there."

"Me too. Do it." She's wiggling around, her hands moving down from my shoulders to my belt. I watch her intently as she unbuckles my belt, then pops open the button on my jeans.

When I hear that zipping sound, I hold my breath until I feel her little hand slide inside my briefs and that's when I throw my head back and moan. "I love your hands on me. Fuck."

"Help me, Sig."

Setting her feet on the floor, I push my pants down as she kicks her shorts off to the side. "Tank. Off."

With an eye roll and a smirk, she lifts the tank off, leaving her completely nude.

"So beautiful." I reach out and pluck one hard nipple.

I can tell she's impatient, especially when she moves closer to me, lifting one leg up and around my hip. "Now, Sig."

"As you wish." I wrap my palms over her bare ass and lift her again. With her back against the door and her legs wrapped tightly around me, I feel my cock at her entrance. With a thrust of my hips, I'm in. Deep. "Oh, fuck." There's no hesitation, no foreplay, no lingering. This is fucking against a door in its purest form. I don't recall ever fucking with such speed or intensity before this. I'm concentrating so hard. I don't want to come before she does. "Touch your clit, babe."

She doesn't hesitate. Her hand reaches down between us. I stare as she works herself into a dick-clenching orgasm. She's squeezing so hard, I can't hold mine at bay anymore. I press all the way in and release myself inside of her—deep into her fucking womb.

CHAPTER SEVENTEEN

Molly

IF I COULD PUNCH myself in the face, I totally would, because A) I fucked Sig again and B) I fucked Sig without a *freaking* condom. Maybe I don't need to punch myself. Perhaps I should just pound my face against the door that we just did it against. Talk about poetic justice.

"Stop overthinkin' it, babe."

Okay, maybe I shouldn't punch *myself*.... "I overthink every-thing. Get used to it."

"I intend to get used to all of your quirks and idiosyncrasies."

No. No-no-no. This is too much too soon. "Sig..."

Sig's buckling his belt up as he says, "I'm goin' home."

He's going home? Why is that so disappointing?

CHAPTER EIGHTEEN

Sig

I DIDN'T GO THERE to fuck her. Not gonna lie, though, I was hopin'. But now that it's done, I feel regret. No, not regret for having her again. Regret because I should've given her more time to think about everything. Now she's going to add *impatient horndog* to the list of things she doesn't like about me. I scoff aloud as I enter my house. My house. Not home.

"It won't be home until they're here with me."

Shit. I need advice about her, but I've already heard from Keeton on the matter and from Eric. I think they both support me in this, but they're skeptical. *Me too.* If only Adam were here. As fucked-up as that sounds, if he could be a ghost for just a minute or two, maybe he'd tell me what to do.

Kicking off my boots at the door, I head into my kitchen. Opening the fridge, I see one lone beer. I pick that up, twist off the cap, and throw it back. I had a couple of beers at Burke's place, but not enough to impair me in any way. I kinda wish I'd had more. I could use some impairment right about now.

Flopping down on my couch, I contemplate my next move. The only thing rolling around in my head is showering and sleeping, but that sounds like a lot of fucking effort right about now. I'm tired, sure. But hands down, the thing I'm feeling most is lonely. "I shouldn't have left." I should have bulldozed my way into her house and stayed there. She'd have let me, I know it.

I move until I'm lying on my couch, beer in hand. I bought an extra-long sofa so I could do exactly this: kick back, have a beer, and watch a game while bein' completely lazy. I've got two out of the three things going on right now. With a sigh, I set the beer on my coffee table, put my hand behind my head as a makeshift pillow, close my eyes, and do whatever I can to find some peace about Molly.

I MUST'VE FALLEN ASLEEP, because I wake up on my couch a little disoriented. Looking up at the clock on the wall, I see it's just past midnight. Rubbing my eyes, I push myself up so I'm sitting on the couch. "Time for bed."

On my way to the hallway that leads to my room, I see light coming through my living room window. Light that's coming from Molly's place. If her lights are still on, it means she's still up. I stare at that light. "She needs time," I mumble.

Time sucks.

CHAPTER NINETEEN

Molly
  One week later

WE'RE CELEBRATING the release of my sister-in-law Lainie's newest book, called *Snake: An Archfiends MC Novel*. Each of her books is about one of the guys from her fictitious motorcycle club. She's been slowly making a name for herself as a romance novelist in the MC genre. I've read a couple of her books and they're good. It's just....

I shiver, thinking about the day I overheard them talking in her little office that sits directly across the hall from mine. I didn't mean to hear them. The place was extra quiet. Anyway, it went a little something like this.

> **Lainie:** *Keeton, I need help with a scene.*
> **Keeton:** *Oh, yeah? What's the scene?*
> **Lainie:** *Well, they do it in the shower.*

Keeton: *We've done it in the shower. What's different this time?*
Lainie: *This time she's on her knees.*
Keeton: *Babe... grab your shit. We're goin' home right now.*

I can still hear her tinkling giggles as they ran—yes, ran—out the back door of the shop. That was all I could take, so I covered my ears and did what any self-respecting sister would do: I chanted *la-la-la-la-la-la-la* over and over until they were gone. It's why I skip the dirty parts of her books. TMI. Sorry Lainie.

No matter; I'm happy for Lainie's success. I know it hasn't been all fun and games. Getting her name out there takes more than just writing. She spends as much time promoting herself with social media and other stuff as she does writing. Keeton has been an amazing husband and support for her. He wants her to hire someone to do her PR, but she says she likes to stay connected to her fans by doing it herself. I can see both sides of that.

Looking around the brag room, I notice it's set up much like Maddy's birthday party, only this one is for adults only. The décor is all done in black and silver. There's a giant poster of the book cover. Damn, it's hot. The model on the cover could star in some pretty hot dreams if I let him. I know she hired the guy through a modeling agency in Phoenix. She picked well. I wish I could have been at the shoot. Maybe I'll invite myself along next time. I scan the room, seeing all of the Palmer sisters in attendance. Their husbands seem to be here as well. There are a handful of people I don't recognize. They're probably book people. I'm sure I'll get a chance to meet everyone by the end of the night.

"Hey, stranger."

I smile and turn to my best friend. "Hey, Deb." I wrap the

arm that's not holding my glass of prosecco around Deb's shoulders. "You look pretty." And she does, in a flowy dress that wraps around her waist.

"So do you. Nice tits," Deb cackles.

I look down at my chest and quickly adjust my dress. "You made me buy this."

"Yeah, because it makes your tits look amazing."

"Shut it. Yours are bigger," I nod toward her chest. "You're not showing yet, though." Deb and Rob finally told Rob's kids about the baby. Deb was really worried they'd be upset about it. "Everything good with the Palmers?"

"Great. They welcomed the news with open arms. It makes it feel real now."

"Real? How so?"

"With me and Rob. I think he wants to move our relationship to the next level."

"Do you?"

Deb turns to me, her smile breathtaking. "I've never wanted anything more in my life. How did I get so lucky to meet him?" Her eyes seem to be getting a little watery.

"Oh, hon. I'm so happy for you."

Sniffling, she wraps her arms around me giving me a tight hug. "Me too. Now we just need to get you sorted."

"I'm sorted just fine."

Deb pulls back and nods behind me. "Who is that with Sig?"

I turn my head and stare. A woman who could be best described as pin-up gorgeous has her fucking hand on my man.

What the hell? *My man?*

I slowly turn my body until I'm facing them. Deb grasps my forearm and squeezes. It feels like support, but she could also be urging me to do something about it.

The woman, a buxom brunette, is leaning so close to Sig, her huge breasts practically swallow up his arm as she whispers into his ear. I watch as Sig laughs at whatever the fuck she just said. And not just laugh. He threw his big, red head back and laughed deep. It's a ridiculous laugh and enough of an opening for the woman to move closer. Now her entire body is pressed against his, and do you want to know the fucking kicker? His hand is on *her* back.

He's. Fucking. Touching. Her.

"You gonna stand here and take that?" Deb isn't the kind to stand idly by and let someone encroach—on her man or her business.

Turning away from him and the bitch he's with, I glare at Deb. My face suddenly feels hot and my teeth are clenched. I'm spitting mad. This time last week, the man was fucking me against my front door, saying a whole lot of bullshit, apparently. I should ignore it. I should just let things be the way they've been this week—normal. We worked together like normal. He mowed my lawn and took our trash to the curb, like normal. We waved at one another, and Maddy hung out with him like normal. So, why should I assume anything he said or did a week ago matters now? He can bring a date to this thing if he wants to. It's none of my business.

My head turns back once again just as Sig leans down and says something in her ear.

"Are you really going to sit back and watch that shit?" snaps Deb. "That bitch needs to go. If you don't do it, I will."

"No. You're pregnant."

"So? I'm not gonna raise a pussy. He or she might as well get used to it."

My God, Deb is as furious as I am.

"Well?" she asks, tapping her foot on the concrete. "What's it gonna be?"

I nod my head as my nostrils flare. "You're right. You're

abso-fucking-lutely right." Handing her my now-empty glass, I move quickly. The click-clack of my three-inch heels is extra loud on the concrete as I stomp toward him. At about three feet out, Sig must hear me, because he lifts his head in time to see me stop, place my hands on my hips, and glare.

He smiles. "Oh, hey, Molly. You havin' fun tonight?"

I snort, then ask, "May I speak with you for a moment?" I glare at the bitch who's still got her claws in his arm. "Privately."

"Uh, sure." He looks at the woman. "Nice talkin' to you, Tonya."

Oh, sure. Of course her name is *Tonya*.

I turn on my heels and start marching through the large open room toward the hallway that leads to my office. I turn my head to make sure he's following me. He is. His eyes are on my ass, but that's okay as long as he's with me.

Pulling my office key out of my bag, I unlock my door and push it open. I motion for him to enter first. As he does, he gives me a little smile.

He doesn't say "darlin'" or "babe." I hate that. Stepping into my office, I flip on the light switch, shut the door, and lean back against it. With my hand behind me, I engage the lock on the knob. We're alone.

Stepping toward him, I don't stop until my body is pressed up against his. "You've got a lot of nerve."

Sig's right brow arches. "How so?"

"Bringing a date tonight."

He smirks. The asshole smirks. "Jealous, darlin'?"

And there it is. "No," I scoff.

With a gentle finger, Sig pushes some hair from my cheek to behind my ear. "I think you are. And it's adorable."

"I'm not fucking jealous. I'm pissed. Who was that slut? Did you bring her just to make your point?"

"Babe, I..."

"You what?"

I feel his palm slide down my back until it's resting on my ass. God, his hands.

Two can play at that game. I move my hand in front of me until it's resting on the zipper of his dark dress pants. He looks hot tonight in his charcoal gray suit, white shirt, and no tie. When I feel how hard he is, I wrap my fingers around his shaft. I give it a little squeeze, then ask again, "Did you bring her to make me jealous, Sig?"

"Darlin'," he says, his voice going down an octave.

I slide my palm against his hard-on. He's making a growling noise, which only turns me on more. "This cock..." I use more pressure on him as I run my palm up and down. "...is mine."

With a grunt, Sig responds, "Yeah, it is. What're you going to do with it?"

What am I *not* going to do with it? Instead of talking, I look up into his eyes as I move down onto my knees.

"Jesus," Sig groans.

"I locked the door." Unbuckling his belt, I undo his button, then unzip him. I grasp the waist of his pants and pull them down slowly, letting my nails drag over the skin of his lean hips. When they're down to midthigh, I move my hand to his shaft. "You want me to suck your cock, Sig?"

"Jesus, fuck... yes."

Licking the tip that's glistening with precum, I swipe my tongue over him once, twice, three times. I push up until my mouth is directly over his tip. "I'm going to blow your mind." God, when did I get so cocky? No pun intended.

"Blow me, Molly. Suck me. Please, Jesus." Sig sounds sort of desperate. "Put that gorgeous mouth on me."

Making sure we're on the same page, I look up at him once more. "Tonya doesn't get this cock, Sig. It's mine. You get me?"

"Fuck. It's yours. It's always been yours. I don't even know her."

I blink a few times. Perhaps I overreacted? No matter; I'm making my point tonight. Sliding my mouth over him, I hum as I move down as far as I can go. With my hand on his base, I work both my mouth and hand so they're moving in sync. Reaching out, I take Sig's hand and place it on my head.

"Fuck. This is what fantasies are made of, woman."

I knew he'd like that.

Concentrating on my work, I push down over him, sucking and licking as I move up his shaft. The man is heaven. He tastes salty and musky. I always liked going down on... Nope. I'm not bringing him into this. This is between me and Sig right now. Forcing myself back into a rhythm, I feel Sig's hand as it moves through my hair. I totally expected him to hold my head so he could control this, but that's not what he does. He's gently stroking my head as I stroke his. Ha! Did you see what I did there? A little play on words?

With my hand on his upper thigh, I feel him tense. Panting, he says, "I'm close. You should stop."

Pulling my mouth away, I use my hand to pump him. When he comes, I feel his entire body vibrate as he spurts. I end up with some on my dress and a little on my neck. He must've noticed, because he reaches for a couple of tissues from the box on my desk and starts to clean me up. Taking the tissue, I smile up at him. "I got this." I nod to his softening cock. "You need some too."

Once we're cleaned up and Sig is dressed again, he pulls me into his arms and kisses the top of my head. He's quiet. Too quiet. So, I ask him, "What's wrong?"

"I'm scared."

He's scared? Sig Engel, Army Ranger, is scared? "Of what?"

He releases a deep breath. "I'm scared you didn't mean what you said."

Leaning back, I stare into his golden eyes. "Which part? That you'd better fucking stay away from Tonya...?"

He shakes his head.

"Oh, the part where I said your dick was mine." I chuckle, but Sig isn't laughing.

"I want this, Molly. I want it all with you and with Maddy. Don't toy with me."

"Wow." I pull away. "I knew I gave good head, but that's..."

"Stop!" Sig says angrily. "You're making light of all of this, Molly. If you were just jealous and had to prove a point, then fuck you." He stomps toward the door. Turning back to me, he isn't smiling. "I love you, but I can't take this tentative bullshit. When you're ready for this, *us*"—he points first at himself, then at me—"call me. Otherwise..." He runs his hands through his hair, hard, almost pulling at it. "Fuck it. I'm out of here."

I watch him open the door, step out, then shut it behind him as I stand by and watch him go. The only word that leaves my mouth is, "Sig."

CHAPTER TWENTY

Molly

US?

Is there an *us?* God, I can't process any of this. So, I do what feels natural. Since Maddy is at her grandparents' for the night, I return to the party and proceed to get shit-faced.

BAD IDEA. *Very* bad idea. The hangover from hell is upon me, and I've got no one to blame but myself. The daylight streaming in hurts, but it's the least of my problems, because there seems to be a strange hand on my ass. Opening my eyes, I blink, attempting to get my bearings. I know one thing. It's not my bedroom, but I recognize it. Rolling over, I feel the sheet fall away from my body as cool air hits my skin. Looking down, I see I'm still wearing my bra and panties. I guess that's something.

I'm not naked. Since I'm in Sig's bed, I don't think it's necessarily a good thing.

"How do you feel?" His voice is scratchy. Sexy.

"Like someone ran over me, then had their dog bite me repeatedly."

Sig chuckles. "That's one I haven't heard before."

"That's 'cause I made it up right then."

"Ah, I see."

Rolling over until I'm facing him, he's looking back at me. He doesn't look mad, but he doesn't look happy either. "How…"

"Deb called me. Said you were drunk as a skunk and would I come get you."

Deb. My former best friend. "Ah, well, I'm sorry about that. I know you probably didn't want to—"

"I love you, Molly. No matter how pissed off I am, I'd always make sure you were safe."

"Oh." I don't know what it was about his last statement that made me do it, but I break into tears right that second. I can't contain the sobs, and I don't really want to. Maybe I'll just cry my hangover away.

"Baby," Sig says sweetly. Pulling me into his arms, he holds me close to his chest. I feel his hand run over the top of my head gently. "Don't cry, darlin'."

He can tell me to stop all he wants. It's not gonna happen. Not for a while, anyway.

I lay my head on Sig's shoulder and breathe deep.

One of Sig's arms is wrapped around my back, his palm on my hip. The other hand is on the knee closest to him. Ever so slowly, Sig rubs my leg from my knee down to my foot. It's such a soothing gesture, I let my body relax at his touch and then his words. "It's gonna be okay, sweetheart."

"Do you really think he'd want me here with you? Like this?" I can't help asking. It's the root of my issues with Sig and me. It's so surreal. I just can't see my Adam being happy about me lying in Sig's bed, doing the things we've done.

"Yeah. I know he'd be okay with it."

Opening my eyes, I look into Sig's. "How? How do you know?"

Sig kisses my mouth softly. He's staring at me, and I can practically see his brain working. He's got something else to say to me. He's hesitating, though.

"Tell me."

"We talked a lot about you."

I swallow hard. "That-that day?"

"All the time. Every chance he had, he'd talk about you, the baby, Keeton, and Eric. He loved you all so much. But mostly he talked about you—funny stories, sad stories, you name it."

He's stalling. Now all I need to do is wait for the real answer. What did he say *that* day?

"Babe."

I swear I see his heart beating in that vein at the side of his neck, and it's beating fast.

"You sure you want to hear this?"

I nod. I don't think I could talk if I wanted to.

He kisses me softly again. "Okay." He sighs then begins, "He... he asked me..." Sig swallows and then blurts, "He told me to love you."

My mouth opens, then closes, and that repeats half a dozen times. I'm struck dumb, but I finally get it out. "Excuse me?" I push back. I can't get far enough away from him. "What kind of fucked-up shit are you spewing, Sig?"

"Babe." Sig sits up and reaches for me, but I'm not having it. "Think about it. Where we were. What had happened."

"Think about what? That I'd believe, for one second, my husband would just-just..."

"We were goddamn brothers, Molly. He was family to me."

Sig reaches for me, and I let him this time, because his words are rolling around in my head: *Think about it. Where we were. What had happened.*

Emotion starts to climb up from my belly into my throat, making my face heat and my eyes burn. "He really said that, Sig?"

"Yes. He really did. I'd never lie to you, especially about Adam."

Wrapping me up in his arms, he pulls me to him. He has my undivided attention.

"And before you let that beautiful head of yours start to overthink this shit, I'm going to tell you I came here, to Page, to do what I promised. To take care of you and Maddy. Falling in love with you was just a bonus."

He's gazing at me. There's no better word to describe it, and it makes me feel like we're the only two people in this entire world. I stare back up at him, zeroing in on his eyes. I can't believe what I'm seeing reflected. There's no other word to describe it than *love* and Maddy is part of this. The biggest part.

Sig smiles, and a dimple appears on his cheek. A dimple I'm sure I've only ever seen directed at my daughter. "Us. The three of us."

CHAPTER TWENTY-ONE

Sig

WHILE MOLLY ATTEMPTS to shower away the effects of too much booze, I'm in the kitchen making up the perfect hangover breakfast: bacon, bacon, and more bacon. My thoughts aren't on cooking, though. They're on the conversation we just had in my bed. At the end, I felt somewhat optimistic, but something tells me this discussion isn't over. I'm betting her thoughts are all jumbled. I don't doubt that she'll withdraw again. It seems to be her MO after our intense conversations. And this morning's talk was, by far, the most intense. I can practically read her damn mind. She'll wonder if I only love her because Adam told me to. God, *women*. You can't *make* someone love you. You either do or you don't. Shit. People have written songs about it. I'm sure there are books with the same theme. You either you do, or you goddamn don't.

And I definitely do.

CHAPTER TWENTY-TWO

Molly

AS WARM WATER sluices down my body, I roll my head back to rinse out the soap. My hair and body are going to smell like Swagger, but it can't be helped. I've got to use what's on hand. I have to admit, though, I like the smell. It's Sig's scent— masculine without being overpowering.

When I'm squeaky clean, I give my hangover some thought. Yes, my head still hurts, and I think I did something to my toe last night, because it hurts like a house on fire. Looking down, I notice the toenail looks a little wonky.

Did I kick something?

Who knows? I'll ask Deb about it.

Out of the shower, I find a towel on his special towel bar and moan when I feel how warm it is. "I need one of those." Wrapping up in the cozy warmth, I find a brand-new toothbrush in a drawer in his vanity. In the second drawer, I discover a hairbrush, so I use that to work the knots out of my hair. I feel like a new person.

Rummaging through his drawers for something to wear feels wrong somehow, but I'm doing it anyway, because I can't put that dress and heels back on. The bottom drawer is filled with T-shirts. Score! Once I slide one on, I'm happy to report that it goes down to my knees. I'm covered in case he has any visitors this morning.

I stare longingly at his bed. Napping sounds good, but the scent of bacon cooking draws me out of the bedroom and into his kitchen. "Mm, that smells delicious."

"You want eggs and toast?"

"Toast." The first thing I notice when I round his kitchen island is Sig is wearing only his boxer briefs. They're gray today. His ass flexes every time he flips a piece of bacon. I'm sort of mesmerized by it.

"You done starin' at my ass, darlin'?"

"No." Then I giggle. Moving further into his kitchen, I look for a toaster. I spot it next to the coffeepot that's brimming with caffeinated goodness. "Where's the bread?"

Sig steps over to me and gets an inch from my face. I watch as he sniffs the air. "You smell like me."

"Yeah, well..."

"And you're wearin' my shirt."

"Sorry..."

He doesn't let me finish. "You're making my cock hard, babe."

I look down at his underwear and can't help noticing he's right.

"Sorry?" I shrug. *Not sorry.*

"Bread's in the cupboard above the toaster. Cups are there too. Cream is in the fridge and sugar in that dish next to the coffee maker."

Wow, he's thought of everything. Almost. "Butter?"

He's turned back to the bacon when he mutters, "Fridge."

Gathering up everything I need, I make toast for both of us. "You want coffee?"

"Sure."

Filling his cup, I'm trying to remember how he takes his. He must like cream, because he's got some in the refrigerator.

"Black, babe. Three sugars."

The man is a frigging mind reader. "Then why do you have cream?" Ha! Got him.

"Because you like it."

Oh. Wow. I'm facing his back as I think about what he just said. In barely a whisper, I say, "Thanks."

"No problem, Molly."

I sip my coffee quietly as he works, until he asks, "When does Maddy get home?"

"Three. I'm meeting Carmen and Mike at the coffee shop for the exchange." I snort. "It makes it sounds like we're criminals."

Ignoring my humor, Sig declares, "I'm going with you."

"Okay. Sure." Odd, but okay.

Sig places the plate of bacon on the table. I follow him with four slices of toast and my own coffee. His is already on the table. I sit first and expect him to sit across from me, but he doesn't. He sits next to me, placing his palm on my thigh the second his ass hits wood. "I'm glad you're here, Molly."

The sincerity in his voice and eyes makes me feel something I haven't felt in a long-ass time. I feel loved, desired, wanted, and, best of all, cared for.

"I know I'm a hot mess, Sig, but I'm glad I'm here too. Thank you for taking care of me last night."

I stand, pushing out the chair. As I approach, Sig pushes his chair back and widens his legs. I move between them and wrap my arm around his shoulders, sitting on one of his thick thighs. Without another word, I lean close and kiss his mouth. "I'm scared too."

"I know, Molly," he whispers. "We'll get through this together. One day at a time."

Nodding, I move in for another kiss. "You like how I smell?"

Chuckling, Sig pats my lower back. "Let's eat. Then I'll show you what you're doin' to me this morning."

I reach out and pick up two slices of crispy bacon and hold one in front of his mouth. Sig bites down, his eyes never leaving mine.

"Mm, good," I say as I chew on my own slice. "Bacon is the cure-all for hangovers."

Sig leans forward, picking up another slice of bacon. This time he holds it in front of my mouth. Instead of biting, I use my tongue and lick the tip.

With a growl, Sig tosses the bacon back on the table. "You don't play fair, woman."

I feel myself being lifted into the air. I'm flipped until he's got me over one of his shoulders. Giggling, I ask, "What're you doing?" I know what he's doing.

"Temptress. I'm taking you to bed."

Temptress. I like that.

"Let's do it doggy style this time."

Sig laughs and says, "As you wish, princess."

Princess too? Wow, my morning is getting better and better.

CHAPTER TWENTY-THREE

Molly

"MAMA!" shouts my little girl from across the coffee shop. She doesn't get up from the table—probably because she's coloring. You can't interrupt an artist at work, am I right?

Weaving in and around tables, I make my way over with Sig in tow. When we reach the table, everyone is silent.

Oh, right.

"You all remember Sig Engel, right?"

"Of course," Carmen says sweetly. Stepping over to him, she holds her hand out to shake. "It's nice to see you again, honey."

Honey? I'd like to laugh at that, because of all the adjectives I'd use to describe Sig, *honey* isn't one of them. Well, he is sweet when he wants to be.

"You too, Mrs. Barone."

Mike approaches with his hand extended. "Son."

"Mr. Barone."

"Call me Mike, son."

"And I'm Carmen," she chirps.

"Mike, Carmen," Sig says with a seriousness I've never seen before. "Nice seeing you again."

"Thig!" shouts Maddy like she just realized we were there. "Wook." She holds up a picture of three people and a dog. Again. It seems to be a theme with her. Only this time, I see the hair color on the man. It's red.

We all stare at the picture in silence. I realize how that must look to Carmen and Mike. Like their son has been replaced by a giant red-haired man. A red-haired man standing next to me. Without another thought, I blurt, "I can explain."

Mike and Carmen's eyes move from the drawing, to Sig, then to me.

Mike speaks first, and it nearly knocks me over in shock. "It's about damn time."

"Hear, hear," says Carmen, clapping. "It's been long enough, sweet girl. Adam wouldn't want you doing this alone."

"Carmen. It's not—"

Sig doesn't let me finish. "Yes, it is, Mr. and Mrs. Barone. I love Molly and Maddy. I have for some time, but this thing with Molly and me is recent. We meant no disrespect to you or to Adam's memory."

"Oh, son." Mike steps closer to Sig. Before I know it, he's wrapped up in Mike's arms. When he lets my big guy go, he adds, "You're Angel, aren't you?"

"How did you know that?" I squeak.

Looking at me, Mike winks. "I was stationed in Germany for several years. I took it upon myself to learn the language. I recognized the word. Plus, I've read Adam's letters a number of times since he passed, and Angel was mentioned in them repeatedly."

I'm still speechless, but more so when Mike hugs Sig again. "Welcome to the family, son."

I'm about to cry, but Sig beats me to it. Wrapping Mike up in his own hug, Sig's eyes are filled with tears as he says, "Adam talked a lot about you and Mrs. Barone. He said you were his hero, sir." Turning to Carmen he adds, "And that you were the sweetest, kindest mom in the world."

Oh, shit. It's become a fucking sob-fest. The only person not crying is Maddy, who is totally oblivious to the scene before her. I guess that's a good thing.

After that, we all sit around the table and drink coffee like we've been doing it for years. It's comfortable. *Too* comfortable. Now all I can do is wait for the other shoe to drop.

CHAPTER TWENTY-FOUR

Sig

SHE'S TOO CALM. After everything that went down in the coffee shop earlier today, I thought we'd get back to the car, or at the very least, home, and she'd lose it. But that's not the case. Instead of losing her shit, she calmly unpacked Maddy's bag, which contained mostly toys since Carmen and Mike apparently have a collection of clothes for her. As Maddy immediately began coloring at their small dining table, Molly started making dinner.

So, what am I doin'? I'm standing around clenching and unclenching my hands because I feel like I need to do something. Anything. Whether that's fixing something or coloring with Maddy, it doesn't matter. Honestly, what I really want to do is go into the kitchen and wrap her up and hold her, because the storm that's brewin' in my woman is coming, and I'd much rather head it off before it hits. So, damnit, that's what I'm doin'.

On my way into the kitchen, I stop and check out Maddy's

newest drawing. It's a dog. "I think you're trying to tell us somethin', aren't you, sweetie?"

"Huh?" she asks, distracted by her work.

"Nothin'." I run my hand over her hair and smile. She's got her mama's hair.

Moving past the table, I step up to the kitchen entry. It's small. This room really does need to be opened up, but I think it'd be a waste. It won't be long 'til we're living together, either at my place or at the place we build. At least that's what I'm hoping for. Lost in thought about all that, I almost miss the sniffle. Before she even notices me, I move in behind her and wrap her up in my arms. She releases a shuddering breath.

"Darlin', it's okay. No one is forgetting about Adam. They just want you to be happy. We'll go as slow as we need to go, babe. No rush."

Releasing a watery sob, she turns in my arms. "That's just it, Sig," she says, wiping the moisture from her nose. "I don't want to slow down. I'm happy that Carmen and Mike approve of us."

"Then why are you cryin'?"

"Because..." A torrent of tears pours from her eyes. "It's l-like I'm just letting him go all of a sudden. I feel so bad because I'm happy and I shouldn't be. I should be sad because he's not here."

I pull her close to me and run my palm up and down her back. I let her cry until she's quieted down. "I get it. You feel guilty, and that's normal, natural."

"I know," she says, sniffling.

"It's okay to feel all those things. It's part of the process of healing. We'll never forget Adam. We'll never stop talking about him. I'm not him. I'm well aware of that, and I'll never ask you to stop loving him, because that's not what this is about. He was our family. We never turn our backs on family."

"Oh, Sig."

The crying has started up again. "Shh, babe. It's okay."

"I don't think it'd be right for Maddy to call you Dad or Daddy. Is that okay?"

Shit, I never gave that a thought. "I'm Sig. Maybe later she'll come up with another name for me, like Big Red." I chuckle. "We're lucky."

Looking up at me, I can't help noticing that her pretty face is red and a little puffy from crying. "How are we lucky?"

"We're lucky because we both loved him and we can both share our stories about him with her. She'll never be able to forget about him, ever."

"Oh, Sig." And the sobbing starts again.

"Come on. Let's go sit on the couch."

"Dinner..."

"We'll order pizza."

"From Giovanni's?"

"Sure. Whatever you want." I take her by the hand and lead her over to the couch. Sitting first, I pull her onto my lap.

"Hey," says Maddy with one sassy hand on her hip. "Mama, you can't sit on Sig's lap. You're too big."

"Come on over, kiddo. We can all get cozy and watch a movie."

"*Tangled!*" she shouts at the top of her lungs.

Wiping her nose, Molly adds, "And we're ordering pizza."

"A party!" Maddy shouts again.

"Absolutely." I wrap my arm around her back and squeeze Molly's arm. "This is a celebration."

PERFECTION. That's what this is. I'm sitting on Molly's couch with my woman asleep, her head in my lap, while Maddy is tucked into my side, asleep as well. My heart feels like it's doubled in size since I sat down with my two girls.

It's a simple thing. Some might even call it mundane to be hanging out on the couch watching an animated movie with your family, but for me, this is fucking everything.

A surge of emotion fills my belly, moving up into my chest, my throat, to my face. There, my cheeks heat and my eyes burn. "So fucking perfect," I whisper so they don't wake up. That's the last thing I want. Honestly, I could sit here forever.

"I should put Maddy to bed," says a groggy Molly.

And bam, it's over.

"I've got her." Sliding out from under Molly's head, I gently pick up mini-Molly and carry her upstairs to Princess Maddy's Bedroom. That's really what it's called. It says so on the door. The little tyke doesn't wake up as I pull off her little sneakers. Laying her on the bed, I pull a blanket over her and walk backward to the door.

"She's something, isn't she?" Molly still sounds half asleep. I turn and smile. I didn't even hear her come upstairs. She's like a ninja.

"She is that."

"Here, she needs her nightlight on." She steps around me and bends over to do something, and my eyes make a beeline to her sweet ass.

Not now, Sig.

Molly pulls the door shut, and we stand in the dark hallway. The only glimpse of light is coming from the streetlights shining through a nearby window. Without thinking, I run my finger across her cheek. "I'm going to head home."

"Oh?" She looks up at me, and I can see disappointment.

"I'm not sleeping in Adam's bed." I shouldn't bring it up, but I can't keep that to myself either.

"It's not Adam's bed. Our bed was used when we got it, so

it's in the spare bedroom now. That bed downstairs," she points toward the stairway leading down, "has only slept me and Maddy."

I'm still not sure. "It's the symbolism," I grumble.

"Sig." She steps closer. "Are we doing this or not?"

I nod. "Fuck, yes."

"Then, let's not half-ass it. Let's not confuse things. Either you're in or you're not."

I chuckle, because those are fine words coming from the most stubborn woman in the world. "So, I'm moving in?" I smirk. I know she's not ready for that.

"Not yet. And if we do decide to live together, I think your place is better. I like the open floor plan and your updated bathroom." It's Molly's turn to smirk.

"Then what would we do with your place? Sell it?"

"No," she says quickly. "I can't sell it. But I could rent it out."

"Okay." I wrap my arms around her and pull her closer. "What if we built out on that land?"

Molly pulls away from me, and it causes me to stiffen up. I went too far. When she takes me by the hand and leads me into her bedroom, I'm surprised. "Come to bed. We can talk then. I'm dead on my feet."

I sit on the side of the bed as she prepares for sleep. It's fascinating to watch her routine. She pulls a nightgown out from beneath a pillow. I watch as she strips down to her panties, then she slips on the conservative nightgown. The sexy-as-fuck conservative nightgown——on her. On anyone else, I'd call it grandmotherly. Reaching back, I pull my tee off and place it on the end of the bed. Next, I stand and undo my belt and unzip my jeans and let them fall to the ground. Standing in only my boxer briefs, I wait for her to show me which side of the bed is hers. When she chooses the left, closest to her bedroom door, I sit down on the other side. It feels strange. I know what she said in the hallway, that this particular bed didn't belong to Adam, but it still feels like sacrilege to be in this bed, in this room, in this house, with her.

"You're going to need to let it go," she says, rolling over to face me.

I still haven't moved from sitting on the side of the bed. "What are you talking about?"

"Adam isn't here with us."

The fuck he's not. "I know."

"Listen." She sighs and sits up so she can lean her back on the headboard. "It's weird. Yes. So, let's do this. Whenever we're here, in this bed," she pats the pillow next to her. "We sleep."

"Only sleep," I mutter and arch a brow.

"Then..." She pauses. "When we're at your house..."

"Yeah?" I ask, my brow moving up so far into my forehead it hurts.

"We do *other* things."

I hope she means fucking. "Can we go to my house now?" I chuckle.

"Not tonight." She looks at me with a serious expression. "Do you have a room for Maddy to sleep in?"

Shit. When Molly sees Princess Maddy's Bedroom á la Sig's house, she's probably going to freak the fuck out. The word stalker comes to mind, but I'd prefer to call myself prepared. It's not the exact replica of her bedroom here, but it's pretty damn close. All she needs to do is move some toys and clothes in there and she's set.

"Yes."

I think I shocked her, because her mouth opens and closes. She watches me so closely, I feel myself get sort of fidgety.

"What aren't you telling me, Sig?"

I look down at my fingernails. They are sort of fascinating right now. "Nothin'."

"She's got a bedroom at your place, doesn't she?"

I turn my body until I've got a knee up on the bed. "Let me explain."

I watch as the most beautiful thing happens. Molly smiles. And not just any smile. She's beaming, so hard her eyes are merely slits. "I love you, Sig."

What the fuck?

"I love you too, babe."

"You made my baby girl a home away from home, didn't you?"

I nod, still not quite sure if this is a setup or not. "I tried."

Molly is up on her knees and in my arms so fast, I almost fall off the side of the bed. Kissing me quickly on the lips, she says, "I can't wait to see it." She kisses me again, softer this time. "Come on, lie down. Let's talk about the house out by Keeton's before I fall asleep."

I wait for her to move back to her side of the bed. Sliding my feet beneath her cool sheets, I lie back on my pillow until I know she's situated. I roll onto my side and scoot as close to her as I can get. Wrapping my arm over her waist, I rest my palm on her belly. "That okay?"

"Uh-huh."

Okay. Good. "So, we're building?"

"Yep."

And then she's out like a light.

Fuck, why did I wait so long for this?

Oh, I remember. She wasn't ready. But she's sure as hell ready now. Thank fuck.

EPILOGUE

Molly
One year later

WHAT A DIFFERENCE A YEAR MAKES. This time last year, at Maddy's third birthday party, I felt like my life was in a never-ending spiral of sadness and misery. Okay, that's a tad dramatic, but close to the truth. But, this year? This year, her fourth birthday is a complete one-eighty. We're having the party in Keeton's brag room again. It seems to be the only space large enough to handle our ever-expanding family. I'll tell you more about them in just a minute. First, I want to tell you about Sig, Maddy, and me.

I guess the biggest news is that we're engaged. All three of us. Sig asked Maddy to be a part of the proposal. He even gave her a special necklace with a tiny ring hanging from it that she wears every single day. He proposed to me two months ago while we were in Las Vegas on a romantic weekend away. I was surprised by the timing of the proposal. We'd talked about getting married several times, but seeing him down on one knee in our suite at the Bellagio Hotel made it all real. I said yes, of course.

Looking down at my pretty ring, I smile. It was his mom's ring. It's a simple band with a solitaire diamond set in the middle. It's not a big rock or anything, but I don't need a big rock. I just need him.

When we got back, we took Maddy out to eat at her favorite restaurant, McDonald's, and he asked her if she wanted to be a family. Without blinking an eye, she shrugged. "Sure," she said, then ate a chicken nugget. And that was that.

Since the proposal, we started the process of building our house near Keeton's place. Sig sold his place, getting top dollar for it, then moved in with us. We used the proceeds from the sale of his home, along with my savings, to break ground on the new place. They've got the entire thing framed up already. It's moving faster than I expected, which is good, because I'm excited to move into the place that's nearly double the size of our current house. Not to mention the main part of the house will be open concept, so I can cook and still interact with my little family. The bedrooms are much larger than our other house, and we'll have huge walk-in closets and attached bathrooms. Even Princess Maddy will have her own bathroom.

Speaking of Princess Maddy.

"When can we eat cake?" she asks with that sassy hand on her hip.

"As soon as people are finished eating." Heck, we're still waiting for a few people to arrive. "And Aunty Deb isn't here yet, so we'll wait until everyone gets here." Since she had her son, she's had trouble getting places on time. No worries. Deb and Rob can be as late as they need to be, as long as we get to see them with their little guy, Wiley. He was born a little early, which freaked my best friend out something terrible, but Wiley is a healthy little guy.

To say Rob was thrilled about his son is an understatement. Don't get me wrong, Rob Palmer loves his girls with his whole heart, but when he glimpsed his son for the first time, I don't think I've ever seen a man so overwhelmed with joy. Rob had all five of his daughters wrapped up in one giant hug at the hospital. It was a sight to behold. I should know, I videotaped the entire scene. Deb was beyond happy too, because now not only does she have two men in her life who think she hangs the moon, but she's also got five stepdaughters, their husbands, and step-grandchildren to make her life complete.

"How about now, Mama?"

I look down at my little peanut. "Honey, asked and answered."

"But, Mommy..."

I'm saved from having to get snippy with the birthday girl when Sig steps in to save the day. Something he does quite often. "Come on, Mad Max, let's get a donut from the donut wall while we wait for everyone else to get here."

Sig surprised her with a large wooden display with four rows of four pegs, each peg holding a stack of four different kinds of sprinkle donuts. What can I say? My man's a genius.

"Yay! Donut wall." Maddy takes Sig's hand and, stepping out in front of him, she pulls him toward the colorful display.

Feeling instantly relieved, I plop my butt into one of the folding chairs.

"You okay, sis?"

I look up at my little brother. "I'm good, Eric."

"How far along are you?"

"Huh?" I'm shocked at his question. Because it's true. We *just* found out though, so there's no way he could have known. "How?"

"You look tired."

"I'm always tired."

"I remember when you were pregnant with Maddy. It's more than tired. So, are you?"

"I am, but don't say anything." Ha! Like that's going to happen. My brothers have big mouths. "We just found out."

"Sure. Your secret is safe with me. But," he winks, "I'll have to tell Vi. I can't keep secrets from my wife."

"Whatever," I grumble. I might as well just announce it. Not that Violet can't keep a secret; she sure as shit can, but why would I ask her to do that? So, without another thought, I stand up and shout, "I'm pregnant!"

I glimpse Sig over near the donuts. He looks shocked at first, but then a broad smile slides over his pretty face. The group that's in attendance claps. The few closest to Sig slap him on the back. Several close to me hug me, one or two shake my hand, and my big brother, Keeton, wraps me up in his arms saying, "So happy for you, Molls." And Keeton *is* happy. He loves having everyone's kids running around, including our newest additions: Keely and Nick's son, Gabriel; Wiley; and Keeton's second child, Audrey, who is the spitting image of Keeton. Needless to say, she's beautiful. Hell, all the babies are beautiful.

With his big arms around me, I nod and do my best not to cry. I'm happy. So damn happy. But I think there's part of me that's always going to be sad. I guess when you lose part of your heart like I did, nothing will make it grow back. The only thing I can do is fill the rest of it with as much love as I can. So, that's what I'm doing.

And since I know he's watching over us, I look up and whisper, *"We'll always love you, Adam. Always."*

～

If you enjoyed Kayt Miller's The Palmer Sisters series,
check out:

VIVIEN JAYNE REGINALD, a.k.a. Reggie, is an enigma. On one hand, she's a confident, talented artist with an impressive art degree under her belt. On the other, she's an insecure woman who never got over her dad walking out on her when she was thirteen. Sure, she's got issues, but Reggie believes the key to happiness is hard work and making art. Not only that, she's convinced the only man she needs in her life is her best friend, Kai.

CARTER CORCORAN IS A CONUNDRUM. The hottest defensive end in the NFL, Carter is big and brawny and has the best sack percentage in the league. Sure, he's a force on the field but off the field? Let's just say he's got a secret. A secret, only his family knows about.

WHEN CARTER TALKS to Reggie at an art exhibit, he meets a kindred spirit; one who understands his need to create. She's not his type. At. All. She's all curves and spunk. Nothing like his normal arm candy. But, the more Carter learns about Vivien, the more he realizes something's been missing in his life. Something real. Now all he has to do is convince Vivien he's worth the risk.

ALSO BY KAYT MILLER

Bedhead

Redhead

Deadhead

FarmBoy

Game Changer

One of a Kind

The Virginia Chronicles

Our of the Blue: The Flynns Book One

Mick'sology: The Flynns Book Two

Vested Interest: The Flynns Book Three

The Importance of Being Ernie: The Flynns Book Four

The Importance of Being Kennedy's: The Flynns Book Five

Quirky Girl: The Flynns Book Six

The Art of the Game

Lainie: The Palmer Sisters Book 1

Agatha: The Palmer Sisters Book 2

Sadie: The Palmer Sisters Book 3

Cortland: The Palmer Sisters Book 4

Keely: The Palmer Sisters Book 5

Violet: The Palmer Sisters Book 6

Molly: The Palmer Sisters Book 7

The Portrait Painter

Hopeful Romantic (Link coming soon.)

Thanks to Margie Dill (Link coming soon.)

The Palmer Sisters Cover Designs
by
Colleen Galligan
galligancolleen@gmail.com

Colleen,
Thank you for all of your hard work
and creativity on the new covers!
I love them! KM

Kayt grew up in the midwest surrounded by a loving family which included three brothers, one sister, and parents who always fostered her creative side.

Kayt wrote her first book when she couldn't find a story about a certain type of a woman and a specific kind of man. She called it *Game Changer* and it couldn't have been a more appropriate title. It changed her life in many ways.

Her goal, as a writer, is to write stories that relate to all of us, to make readers laugh and maybe cry sometimes. Kayt hopes her readers can escape into a fantasy, one that's actually possible. Sure, some of the stories are dubbed "Insta-love" but that's okay. She fell in love with her husband pretty damn fast and with her daughter the second I saw her. So, it's a thing, I swear.

 facebook.com/authorkaytmiller

 twitter.com/kaytmiller1

 instagram.com/kaytmiller1

 bookbub.com/profile/kayt-miller

Thank you so much for reading Molly, Maddy, and Sig's story! When I start a story, it begins with an outline, notes, and lots of crazy thoughts running through my head. When I actually start writing, the characters take over, leading me through the story like they're holding my hand—guiding me. The process is exciting and cathartic. With that said, I hope you enjoy the story.

If you did, please go to my website, www.kaytmiller.com, and join my newsletter so you can be the first to know what's coming up next. And...

Please, leave a review!

Chapter 1: Isabelle

"Mm-mm-mm. They sure don't grow boys like that out east."

My friend and coworker, Rose, and I are both staring at the same man. "Yeah, well, *he's* not the typical Iowa farm boy."

"I think you mean *man*. Farm *man*. Because there's no boy left in that." She points at his backside as he walks down the long corridor away from us.

I snicker at her words because it's what I do when I get nervous. I giggle, snicker, snort, or straight-up laugh out loud. It's my coping mechanism in situations that are too awkward for me to handle. "Even when he was a teen, he looked like that." The tall, dark-haired, muscled, beautiful man in question? Nashville James Watson. But everyone just calls him Nash.

"God, Izzy, how did you not throw yourself at that man back then?" She arches her brow. "Or now. *You're* single."

"Easy. He's my brother's best friend and two years older than me." Not to mention, I was *not* the kind of girl he went with. Cheerleaders and prom queens, those were his type. Actually, he went with one girl that fit both those bills: Ivy DeLucas.

Rose scoffs, "Two years is nothing now. I heard he's single."

"He is." And the last I knew he wasn't looking for anything serious. "I think he's playing the field."

Rose snickers. "*I'd* play in his field...."

"Shh." I giggle. See? Nerves. Whispering, I add, "Someone will hear you." And that's definitely not what we're supposed to be doing on Open House night at our school. "We're professionals." I give her my haughtiest look, nose in the air and everything. "And what about your husband? He's great looking."

"First of all, I love my sexy husband, but it doesn't hurt to look, and two, nobody can hear us way back here." Our classrooms are the last two doors in the main hallway.

Rose is our Special Education teacher, and this is my first year as the Title 1 Reading teacher at Honeywell Elementary School. Heck, it's my first year of teaching, period. I just graduated last spring. I wasn't sure about coming home. I'd hoped to find something in a big city or at least a town closer to civilization, but nothing panned out, and believe me, I tried. Luckily, I grew up in this town and the superintendent is a friend of my folks; otherwise, I'd probably be unemployed or, worse, working as a waitress like I did in college. No thanks.

Truthfully, I'm torn. A small part of me is glad to be back. The other part wishes I'd found a job somewhere else, somewhere nobody already knew me so I could be anyone I wanted to be. I could have been *Isabelle*, but instead, I'm back and I'm still boring old Izzy Harmon.

At least I have a job in my field. That's more than I can say about some of my friends from college. It's great because I love kids and I'm looking forward to working with all these little humans. I know some of them are children of people I grew up with, so that will be good, I guess. For the most part anyway. *Think positive, Izzy.*

It *will* be good.

I'm jolted from my thoughts when I feel my body lurch forward and realize Rose must have pushed me into his path. When he looks down at me, I blush and fumble with words. "Oh." Giggle. "Hi, Nash."

"Hey," he says, walking past me like he doesn't know me. The thing is, he *does* know me. He saw me practically every day for years because Nash and my brother, Isaac, were best friends and as far as I know, they still are. Heck, Nash was Isaac's best man in his wedding. I know because I was there. I was a bridesmaid. I'm pretty sure he saw me there, and Lord knows I haven't changed *that* much. Yes, I've changed a little bit. I started taking a kickboxing class in college and never stopped. I love to kick and punch stuff. Who knew? It helped turn my round, soft body into a curvy soft body. I have a waist, something I never had growing up. But there are things that won't ever change thanks to heredity, and that's okay. I'm embracing my body. I'm built just like my mom, and I happen to think she's gorgeous. Other than that, I'm the same Izzy Harmon he used to ignore back in high school.

You know what, never mind him. I don't need to be recognized by the town's most eligible bachelor and a guy who smells better than I remember, like man and earth. Nope, I don't need him to acknowledge me even though I honestly considered him a friend, sort of. Turns out he's just as snobby and perfect as he was back then. Too good for the likes of me. I snort and can't help saying, "You know, if he'd gotten down off his high horse, his pedestal, once in a while, maybe he would have ended up with a good woman instead of in the mess he's in right now."

"Who are you talking to?" Rose whispers as she side-eyes me.

"Nobody."

I cross my arms in front of my chest and scowl at the little angel who just stopped in front of me. As soon as I see him, I uncross my arms and bend so I'm at his level. He's got to be in second grade. "Hi there. I'm Miss Harmon."

"I know." He's not smiling. "I'm Marcus. I guess you're my new reading teacher."

"I am." I hold out my hand to shake his, but that's a nonstarter. "I'm anxious to get to know you."

Marcus doesn't hold back. "I liked Mrs. Hiller."

Yep, kids are honest. It's so refreshing.

"I know. Me too." I mean that. Mrs. Hiller was an elementary teacher when *I* was in elementary school. But she died last year. She won't be coming back, but I won't say that aloud because that would be rude. Unfeeling.

"Dude, Mrs. Hiller croaked."

I look up to see a boy several years older than Marcus.

"Excuse me...." I'm about to give the older boy a good talking to when a man appears. A suit-wearing man. Something not as common as you'd think in my little town.

"M.J., knock that shit off." When he looks at me, he smiles. "Oh, well, *hello*." He holds his hand out to me. I place mine in his and stare as he slowly bends to kiss my hand. "I'm Max Lang."

"Miss Harmon," I say, rather dumbfounded.

"Miss? Is that your first name?"

I blink a few times, trying to figure out if this guy is serious or if he's trying to be funny. Assuming he's serious, I reply, "Izzy."

He chuckles. "Izzy." He leans in closely, glancing down my shirt. "It's a pleasure."

Not for me, it isn't.

I quickly pull back and cross my arms over my chest again. I knew I shouldn't have worn a V-neck top. But it's Open House, and it's not like it's low-cut or anything. V-necks are just more flattering on me. It's like all the magazines say, highlight your best features. Draw people's attention to that area. And no, I don't mean my boobs. I'm talking about my face and hair. I'm no Ashley Stewart, that's for sure, but I'm not a troll either. Plus, my hair is good. It's dark brown, thick, shiny, wavy, and long. I like my hair.

"These two hellions are mine." Max points to Marcus and the older boy. "My ex-wife is out of the picture." He blinks at me expectantly.

What? Am I supposed to say something? "Oh, I'm...."

And that's when I hear someone yell. I look up to see Nash looking at me. "Max," Nash says, sounding a little angry. "Come on. Let's go."

Max turns to Marcus and the other boy, M.J. "Come on, guys. We're leaving."

My attention is drawn back to Marcus when he shrugs, turns, then walks down the hallway following his older brother. Turning around one last time, Max looks at me and winks. "I'm sure I'll see you again, Izzy." Max then waves as he follows his kids. When he meets up with Nash, they all take off down the hallway toward the main door.

"Jerk," I mutter.

"Max?" snickers Rose.

I look over to her and smile, then laugh. "No. Yes." I'm so glad I get to work with her. We've gotten to know each other quite a bit this summer. The day after I was hired, I started setting up my classroom while she was teaching summer school for extra money. We had lunch together every day, and that's when I filled her in on my old life back here in Honeywell, and since she's been teaching here for several years, she filled me in on school gossip, who to avoid, and who to trust. I had no idea an elementary school could be such a hotbed of drama. It's like a soap opera around here, and the school year hasn't officially started yet.